The End of Science Fiction

Sam Smith

BeWrite Books
www.bewrite.net

Published internationally by BeWrite Books, UK.
32 Bryn Road South, Wigan, Lancashire, WN4 8QR.

A CIP catalogue record for this book is available from the British Library

First published in Australia by
Jacobyte Books, 2000

ISBN 1-904492-70-3

Also available in eBook format from www.bewrite.net

The cover image on The End of Science Fiction is the first picture to show two galaxies in collision and dying in a cosmic firework display light years away from Planet Earth. It's eye-witness proof of scientific theory that these things do happen. Worlds do end. The photograph was taken by the famous Hubble orbiting space telescope and is reproduced by kind permission of NASA.

The End of Science Fiction shortlisted for the **SF Eppie**.

'Smith pulls off his premise skillfully, nay, brilliantly. His prose is clear, smooth and spare. His dialogue reveals the characters' personalities. Even minor characters feel filled out and whole. All in all a most professional job. In a world of book reviews that overstate and overhype, one worries about excess praise, for fear that it will be dismissed. Here I am confounded – there are no faults, no missed notes, no clumsy moves … I always give a writer the opportunity to build the world they are trying to create and if they succeed, the book works for me. In this case Smith succeeds magnificently.'

Miles Archer, Inscriptions Magazine.

'A murder mystery within a disaster novel, The End of Science Fiction is edgy and gripping. Written in present tense, the pace never lets up … The End of Science Fiction has a satisfying and tightly knit plot, and the fast prose style adds a strong sense of drama. Being a disaster novel, it could have easily slipped into melodrama, but Smith keeps the story on an even keel which makes it all the more believable. Long after you've finished reading, you can't help but wonder how you would react, if faced with the same frightening news.'

Ebony McKenna, Sharp Writer Review.

Still dedicated to Dick Szwejkowski,
man of paper

The End of Science Fiction

'All religions promote passivity ... The followers await a saviour or a nirvana – the other side of the bargain if they follow the rules. Which is why all governments are keen to promote religious rather than secular education ...'

Barry Popieluszko. Happy Robot Goes Cosmic: Fire Dragon.

Monday: 10:22

(Scene: Nineteen suited Ministers around the oval table of the Cabinet room. The Prime Minister looks, in turn, at each of the nineteen faces around the table. Circuit completed, he pauses for their full attention.)

Prime Minister: The universe is about to end.

(Members of the Cabinet wait for the Prime Minister to continue. The Prime Minister appears to think that enough has been said. Some Ministers glance across to one another. The Secretary of State for the Arts laughs nervously. Eyebrows are raised, mouths turned down in nonplussed expressions.)

Secretary of State for Trade & Industry: Is that official?

Prime Minister: It's authoritative.

(The Prime Minister defers to the Secretary of State for Defence. The Secretary of State for Defence has dark blue rings around his eyes.)

Secretary of State for Defence: As some of you may have been aware (pause), an argument has been in progress for some time now about the nature of the universe. That the universe was expanding has generally been accepted by most scientific bodies for a good many years.

Secretary of State for the Environment: Was?

Secretary of State for Defence: Was. (Pause.) It is no more. As most of you must be aware, during the last few years evidence has been gathered which proves that the universe has started to contract.

Prime Minister: As I had it explained to me – it's like a piece of elastic stretched to its outermost limit. That elastic has now snapped at both ends and is rapidly contracting.

Chancellor of the Exchequer: This, surely, is common knowledge. Been in the papers for a year or more. Any number of learned books on it. Why should it suddenly concern us here?

Home Secretary: Because no one until very recently realised the speed at which it was happening. Informed opinion was of the belief that the contraction would take place at the same speed, and over the same duration, as the expansion of the universe.

Prime Minister: Back to my elastic analogy. Imagine holding a piece of elastic between your hands, pulling it as taut as you can, then releasing both ends. It snaps towards the centre.

(Members of Cabinet are silent.)

Secretary of State for the Environment: So what will the effect be?

(The question is directed, with hostility, to the Secretary of State for Defence. Secretary of State for Defence has been looking down at a stack of papers on the table before him.)

Secretary of State for Defence: Until now (addresses far corner of room, near ceiling), until the contraction began, we could see only those galaxies less than ten billion light years distant. Any further and they were travelling from us faster than the speed of light and were consequently invisible to us. Those galaxies are no longer retreating from us. Hence, in the last couple of years, the plethora of new star sightings. We are now witnessing something that began at least ten billion years ago. The universe is now contracting. The stars that were at the extremes of the universe are now racing towards its centre. Where they have collided with other stars they have formed bigger stars. Consequently, as the contraction increases in mass, so it will increase in speed. When it reaches us, our sun, our solar system, our world will be incorporated into that mass. And swept away.

Secretary of State for Education: The world will end?

Secretary of State for Defence: Yes.

Secretary of State for the Environment: When?

Home Secretary: In about six, seven days.

(Exclamations from around table. As babble dies, questions are formed, begun, given up.)

Secretary of State for Health: Can we be certain?

Prime Minister: Yes. (Defers to Secretary of State for Science & Technology)

Secretary of State for Science & Technology: Reports have been coming in from all over the world. Americans and Chinese have agreed. The Russians only differ on the timetable.

Chancellor of the Exchequer: What do they say?

Secretary of State for Science & Technology: They think it will be less. Three or four days. The difference is probably due to their sightings having all been taken by satellite.

Foreign Secretary: Whom do you believe?

Secretary of State for Science & Technology: Does it matter?

(Silence.)

Secretary of State for the Environment: May I ask how long the Prime Minister has known?

Prime Minister: For certain? Only two days. The idea takes some getting used to. I'm not sure, yet, that I truly believe it.

Secretary of State for Employment: There could be no mistake?

Prime Minister: I had a look at the stars last night. All is as predicted. Everything is on schedule.

Foreign Secretary: Ours or the Russians'?

Secretary of State for Science & Technology: Both. The difference in the prognosis comes after the third day.

Secretary of State for the Environment: So what do we do?

Prime Minister: Nothing.

Home Secretary: I envisage a certain amount of public disorder.

Prime Minister: We neither confirm nor deny it. That way those who want to believe the world is about to end will believe it. And those who don't, won't. And they will carry on as normal. So, hopefully, some public services will be maintained.

Secretary of State for Trade & Industry: Couldn't that be construed as being rather irresponsible?

Prime Minister: The reverse. If we publicly confirm it, then everyone immediately gives up hope. And everything will collapse in a shambles. If we deny it I doubt that anyone will believe us. All they've got to do is go outside and look at the stars.

Chancellor of the Exchequer: Who, if not us, will tell them?

Prime Minister: The media. The Americans are already breaking the story. British media are bound to follow suit. And don't tell me that we can suppress the news. What powers do we use? D-notices? Declare a State of Emergency? If the papers are convinced that the world is about to end in six days what can we threaten them with? The DPP? When would the case come to court?

Foreign Secretary: What of the American government?

Prime Minister: Noncommital. Declining to comment. To avoid chaos. Their one policy now is not to incite panic. I believe that is also the only course open to us. If, like the Chinese, we had control of our media, then … (The Prime Minister holds open his hands.) Things being as they are, however, were we to ban newspapers, close down television stations and, despite that, the news still got out, then our actions could only be construed as confirmation of that news, and that would guarantee public disorder.

Secretary of State for the Environment: Don't the people deserve a lead from us, their government?

Prime Minister: (Sighs.) Lead them where? Our sole duty now is to prevent a complete breakdown in public order. We can do no more. To confirm the prognosis will be to incite panic. To deny it will be to confirm it; and to cause confusion. And also – and this I feel keenly – it would be a cruel deception. So we will not – I hope you will agree with me – hinder the press in their dissemination of the news. That way, armed with the facts, every individual can meet the end of the world on his or her own terms. I believe that it is our duty. I believe that it is our responsibility. I believe that it is the least we can do. (Pause.) Are we agreed?

(None dissent.)

Prime Minister: I will consult the Opposition leaders, see if I can carry them with me. All must appear as normal.

Foreign Secretary: Does the Palace know?

Prime Minister: Yes.

Secretary of State for Employment: At least the Opposition can't hold us to blame for this.

*'Mass cruelty is inflicted always for The Future, for the Greater Ideal.
Most moral and institutionalised cruelty, that enacted by the individual
too, all is governed by The Future. Of course there will always be
mindless cruelty, that committed out of a lack of compassion, lack of
imagination; reasoned cruelty, however, will always be committed for the
sake of a future.'*

Barry Popieluszko. Raw As Birth: White Swan.

'History is happening every ten minutes.'

Imogen Cooper. Concert pianist: interview Radio Four.

Monday: 11:33

Leaving the Cabinet meeting, Ministers pause to button suit
jackets, look to a looped video on the American leak.

A young official, tense, trembling, leans towards a reporter's
microphone, Capitol Hill in the background.

"… responsible to more than a government department. The
truth should be told. It affects everyone. In six days the world will
end. We have to make our goodbyes. It's the least …" He weeps.

The camera turns towards the female reporter turning towards
it.

Video cuts to interior scene, a function, a drunken white-haired
man, different channel logo. The white-haired man is shouting to
the camera,

"You don't know! You don't know! Over for all of you! All of us. For every goddam one of us …"

An elderly woman in a satiny green dress and a suited young man try to smother him away from the camera.

"Game's over!" he shouts from between their shoulders. "Over!"

Video cuts to newspaper headline.

'Rumour Has It.

Is this the end of the world? Or yet another tired and emotional outburst from a Kansas Senator already well-known to this column …

… Rumour has it that he's not the only one on Capitol Hill prone to such outbursts these latter days of this increasingly hysterical administration …'

Video cuts, loops back to beginning. "… responsible to more than …"

'In law the one solid reason for re-opening a case is that fresh evidence has surfaced ... To reach any judgement, therefore, we have to have information (without all of the information, any judgement is invalid) ... The media thus has to enlighten us, tell us all, so that we may judge our leaders.'

Barry Popieluszko. The Watcher: Kerala Books.

Monday: 19:47

The block of flats is in Victoria, behind the coach station.

In the centre of its underground carpark a square concrete pillar houses the base of the lift shaft and the stairwell. Two unmarked police cars, a squad car and an ambulance are drawn up with their doors open before the lift entrance.

Inside the two unmarked cars are sprawled eight detectives.

Light glows grey-white off the two steep ramps leading up out of the carpark.

A maroon car comes slowly down one of those ramps, stops by the other two cars. Detective Inspector Herbie Watkins pushes himself tiredly out of the maroon car. He walks with the slouch of a tall man, heavy at the hips, rounded shoulders.

Detective Sergeant Jim Nixon, an upright close-cropped man, gets up out of one of the unmarked cars to meet Herbie.

"Forensic and the doc are still up there," he tells Herbie. "Be another half hour yet. Photographer's been and gone. You eaten?"

"No."

"We got some burgers in. Want one?"

Herbie lifts his chin.

From inside the cars the other members of Herbie's team greet him with distant nods. "Chief still here?" he asks Jim.

"Gone. Said it looks straightforward. One way or the other."

Herbie declines to comment on that. "So what do we know so far?" He bites into the squashed burger.

"Deceased is Katherine Helen Soames," Jim reads from his notebook. "Age twenty-eight. Lived alone. Seventh floor. Could have been rape, robbery. She's been done over pretty bad."

"Witnesses?"

"None. But we know he came out through here. They got men decorating the street foyer. Been shut off."

"Checked them out?"

"Office is closed. Found the boss's home address. He's in transit, no mobile, not home yet."

"Who found the body?"

"Old lady next door. Mrs Harris. Came back from giving her dog a walk. Dog ran in there."

"What time?"

"Call was logged 18:09."

Most of the bays in the carpark are occupied. Narrow pavements run up alongside the two ramps to the street. The two tip-up barriers are raised.

"Next of kin?"

"Mother and father. Newbury."

"They been told?"

"Not yet."

"Get the local boys onto it." Herbie signifies the barriers. "Who opened them?"

"Caretaker."

"How they operated?"

"ID card. We being taken off the other one?"

"Temporarily. Leaving a couple of Lord Litchfields up there. Nothing'll happen up there till Friday. No money till then."

Herbie tosses the burger carton into one of the squad cars. "Let's go up."

The lift has doors at either end.

"We in for a late night?" Jim asks as the lift slowly rises. (Slower the lift the wealthier the apartment.)

"Looks like it."

"Shit," Jim says. "We been on all weekend."

"Think of the overtime."

At the seventh floor Herbie and Jim step out onto the landing's moss-green carpet. Opposite the lift are two dark green doors diagonally facing one another. The door to 23 is open. Stairs lead up around the lift to the next landing.

"Stairs go down to the garage?" Herbie asks.

"Been checked," Jim says. "Clean."

"Fire escape?"

"Ain't one. Stairwell's fireproofed." Jim gestures to the stairs. "Neat how they got these flats planned. Entrance on every half-landing, and in the flats split-level. Dining room and kitchen this end; up some steps to bedroom and bathroom. Wouldn't mind one meself."

"You couldn't afford it," Herbie says. "All right to come in?" he shouts through the open door.

The white body lies crookedly against a pale pink settee. A crimson robe has twisted around her. The belt is still knotted. Her forehead, upper face and black hair are coated in blood. On the beige carpet and pink settee are splashes of blood, darker smears on the crimson of her robe.

A grey-suited doctor is crouched beside the body taking swabs. Two forensic men, in blue nylon oversuits, have a stack of brown paper sacks in the centre of the room. The cream telephone has been smashed. Background smell is of cigarette smoke: soaked into the wallpaper, into the curtains. Her hair will smell of that smoke.

A whiff of sweet fruit potpourri too: painted pot been knocked over by the door, orange and yellow contents spilt over the floor, some stepped on, crushed. And another smell ... Perfume? Too sharp. Aftershave? Whose?

"Any ideas?" Herbie asks the doctor from the living room doorway.

"Tried to make it look like rape. They had sex, though, quite some time before she was hit."

"Murder weapon?"

"In the bag."

One of the forensic men is rummaging about in a wastepaper basket.

"Metal figure," he says. "Dancer or something. Plenty of prints."

"What time?" Herbie asks the doctor.

"Four. Just after."

"Trying to phone?" Herbie nods towards the smashed telephone behind the doctor.

"Looks like. Right forearm's fractured."

"Blood splashes?"

"Tried to wash them off." The forensic man indicates the pile of bags. "Got the towel. Plenty of fabric. Suit, I'd say."

"She have a go at him?" Herbie asks the doctor.

"Nails are clean, knuckles unmarked. 'Cept where he hit her hand on the phone. By the amount of blood I'd say she must have struggled a couple of minutes before her heart stopped."

"Anything missing?" Herbie asks the forensic man by the wastepaper basket.

"Purse's been emptied. Plastics are gone. And looks like he took some jewellery. Don't smell right for a robbery though. How many tealeafs you know smoke only half a fag?" He holds up the long stub of a cigarette in a pair of blue plastic tweezers. "And he emptied two ashtrays in here. Four stubs altogether."

"She didn't smoke," the doctor says. "No stains on teeth, none on fingers."

"No fag packets here," the other forensic man tells them. He peels strips of tape from the bedroom doorjamb. "And he washed up his ashtrays and a couple of glasses. Loads of his prints. Big flat thumb. Old and new. Regular visitor. Was here for some time today."

"I concur." The doctor stands to write some labels. "*Cherchez l'homme*."

"How's the old lady?" Herbie asks him.

"Chipper enough. More worried about her dog than anything. Contravenes the lease, apparently."

"I can see her, then?"

"Can you get her prints?" The second forensic man comes down the steps from the bedroom. "Save us bothering her again."

'Men like to challenge the supremacy of Time, lay traps for it by making plans beyond their own lifetimes, put conditions in their wills, set snares beyond their years ... all in an attempt to keep control ...'

Barry Popieluszko. Psychotic Android Eats: Fire Dragon.

'See the man with the hammer smashing grandfather clocks ... He means to kill time.'

Barry Popieluszko. The Watcher: Kerala Books.

Monday: 20:38

Herbie presses the doorbell to number twenty-two. A dog yaps deep in the flat. Doors are opened. Doors are closed.

"Why is it," Jim refers to the doctor and forensic, "they feel they have to be so cheerful?" It is a question that has vexed Jim before. Herbie doesn't reply.

"What do you want?" an old voice asks from behind the door.

"Detective Inspector Watkins." Herbie stoops to the spy-hole, holds up his ID. "Can I have a few words?"

Muttering to herself Mrs Harris unlocks and opens the door. She is one of those old women who seem to have shrunk inside her clothes. "Come in then. Come in."

"Sorry to trouble you again, Mrs Harris." Herbie steps past her. "Just a few things I want to get clear in my mind."

"It hasn't been on the telly yet," she says.

"Might not make it." Jim smiles at her. "You feeling better now?"

"Well, it was a shock."

The flat, compared to the streamlined decor of next door, is a clutter of clashing patterns. Square-patterned carpet, paisley-patterned wallpaper, flower-patterned curtains, circle-patterned upholstery. Fat, soft furniture. The telly has been switched off, ticks and clicks as it cools. The dog whimpers in the kitchen.

"You live here alone, Mrs Harris?" Herbie asks her. The flat has the closed smell of most old people's houses.

"Since my husband died."

"Did you know Miss Soames?"

"Not really. Said hello to her sometimes. She was always rushing in and out."

"Did you ever see her with anyone? A man?"

"I'm not going to have to go to court? Am I?"

"I doubt it. Did you ever see her with anyone?"

"No." Mrs Harris emphatically shakes her head. "Though I know she had someone in there sometimes. Could hear them while I was waiting for the lift."

"Did you hear anything about four this afternoon?"

"Is that when it happened? Poor girl. Such a mess."

"Did you hear anyone in there?"

"I've got this hearing impairment. I don't wear it unless I know I've got company coming. Or for the telly. Or going out. For the traffic you know. It buzzes. Makes me tired."

"And the dog ran in there as you got out of the lift?"

"It was a mess."

"And you came straight in here and called the police?"

"Took me a minute or so to catch Jason. He's so naughty sometimes. Then I had to get my breath back."

"You must have touched things in there?"

"I suppose I must have."

"Would you mind giving us your fingerprints? It washes off afterwards. Only it would help us to eliminate you. That way we'll catch her murderer."

"Do you think he'll be back? I am the only witness."

"Did you see him?"

"No."

"He won't be back."

Jim lays out the charts and inkpad on a coffee table, tells Mrs Harris what he wants to do, takes her hand in his.

"Did Miss Soames have any friends in the flats?" Herbie asks her.

"Not that I know of." Mrs Harris is engrossed in having her prints taken.

"And you never saw her with any man?"

"Once or twice. But I didn't pay any attention. We mind our own business here. Actors, diplomats, film stars, all sorts living here."

"What did your husband do, Mrs Harris?"

"A goldminer. We retired here."

"Here?" Jim smiles at her.

"We lived in this awful place in South America. Jack said he wanted to retire somewhere civilised."

"Would you recognise any of the men you saw Miss Soames with?"

"Will I be called as a witness? It's my dog, you see."

"I doubt it. We mostly need your help with our investigation. When we catch him we'll have enough to get a conviction without your testimony. Would you recognise him?"

"I think so."

"Could you make an identikit?"

"No." She thinks. "No. He looked ordinary. But I'd know him if I saw him again."

"Ordinary? What – young?"

"No. A big man. Respectable. Businessman. You know."

"Middle-aged?"

"I suppose so. It's hard when you're old. Everyone's younger than you."

"He wasn't young?"

"No. He wasn't young."

"Thank you, Mrs Harris. If I do have a suspect, and I need you to identify him, where can I contact you?"

"Oh, I don't go anywhere."

As Herbie and Jim emerge from number twenty-two, the ambulance men are coming out of the lift with their stretcher.

"All yours." The doctor, bag in hand, appears at the door of number twenty-three. "I'll do the PM first thing. Should have my report about ten."

Herbie watches the two ambulance men zip the body into its white bag and strap it to the stretcher. All the violence has taken place by the telephone.

"We're done." The two forensic men drop their brown paper sacks into large black dustbin bags.

"Want a hand with them?" Herbie asks.

"No thanks. You want us to run the prints through records?"

"If you could." Herbie says. "We got a load of doorknocking to do."

The forensic men and the ambulance men struggle with their loads through the door. One of the detectives slips in between them.

"They've found the decorators' boss. The three decorators downstairs were subbies. Got their addresses."

"You check them out, Jim. Persuade them to part with their prints. And run 'em through records. Elimination, that's all. When you done that, clear off home. You get in first tomorrow, though."

Jim takes the addresses off the other detective and leaves.

"As for you," Herbie tells the remaining detective, "I want every flat here visited. Find out where the occupants were between four and six. No, make that between three and six." The detective alters his notes. "If they were here ask if they saw anyone entering or leaving this flat. Anyone in the lift or on the stairs. In the garage. If they saw anyone with a suitcase or a large package. If they had known Miss Soames. If they had ever seen her with a man. Or men. If they would recognise him again. And tell our lot to be civil. Some people here probably think they're important. Don't bother number twenty-two, and leave the caretaker to me. And I want a couple to go across the road to the flats overlooking the carpark entrance. Ask if they saw anyone leaving these flats between four and four-thirty." The detective grimaces. "Worth a try," Herbie tells him.

Alone for the first time in the flat, Herbie looks slowly about him.

The beige carpet owns several blood spots, a damp patch of urine. Plastic splinters from the smashed telephone are scattered over the floor like bone shards. A small antique stand is on its side, the directories in a slewed heap.

On the opposite side of the room, papers and books have been strewn over a glass-topped desk and onto the floor.

Herbie looks out of the window.

This floor is level with the slate roofs of the muddy red buildings opposite. No one would have seen the murder.

Through the open bedroom door a heap of clothes is visible upon the bed where the drawers have been emptied upon it.

Compared to the other rooms the kitchen is orderly and untouched: bottles and pans arranged in order of size in the cupboards. (An habitual burglar would have emptied all the pots and jars.)

Herbie takes the cookery books from their pine shelf by the cooking hobs, looks inside each for an inscription, then holds each book by its spine and riffles the pages. A few recipes cut from newspapers and magazines flutter onto the worktop. He returns the books to their shelf.

Forensic has already been through the waste bin and the sink's waste disposal. In a floor cupboard by the sink is a stack of old newspapers. *The Times. The Standard. The Sunday Times.* The crosswords have been partially completed. Same handwriting as on the shopping list by the fridge.

On the worktop is an electric coffee percolator half full of coffee. Herbie switches it on. In the living room he picks up the telephone directories. None have any messages written on them. He searches for her own telephone book, a jotter. He finds a pen, nothing though on which she could have written.

Her green handbag has been emptied onto the desk. The purse is empty, her credit cards removed from their transparent wallet. Herbie replaces the lipstick, mascara, eyeshadow, mirror in the bag. No driving licence. No keys. The cheque stubs carry a tally of how much she has in her current account. So too the stubs for a deposit account. Not short of a penny. No credit card. Some neatly folded tissues.

He begins to return some order to the glass-topped desk. As he did with the cooking books he turns each book upside down and riffles the pages. Most are scientific publications. A few art books. A lover's gifts. The first pages of two have been torn out.

Herbie crosses to the paintings on the wall, lifts them away from the wall and looks behind them. On the plyboard back of a large watercolour of white lilies is the label of an antique shop. He makes a note of the address. A stack of red drawers below the desk has been pulled out and emptied. A bulldog clip holds a batch of letters. All are from her parents and brother. Other clips hold official correspondence – electricity and gas bills, rates, rent, lease. Her lease includes a parking bay in the carpark. Nothing else refers to a car.

A cardboard wallet holds her passport, birth certificate, NHS card, wage slips and some insurance policies. Beneficiaries are her parents. He does not find a diary or organiser.

In one drawer is a stack of headed notepaper. CAS Ltd, address in Chiswick. He makes a note of the address, finds a list of jobs to be done. Most, he guesses, are to do with work. She is an organised lady. But no diary, no organiser.

A large buff envelope contains a lifetime's photographs. Old schoolgirl and college photographs. Some of her mother and father. Of her brother – from a boy to a man, to a father. Of her nephews and nieces. One studio portrait of her. Herbie puts that aside for the press. In all the recent photographs she has been on her own. He recognises the Scottish islands. The rest he assumes are Mediterranean snapshots. Who held the camera?

A neat and tidy woman. Even on a topless beach not a hair out of place. Even as a child on a rough and tumble family picnic her appearance immaculate. One of her in a bar with a man. The man has long hair, doesn't look like a businessman. Taken, by the fashions, about six or seven years previously. Herbie puts that one aside.

Among the debris of one drawer is an old wire-bound jotter. He flips through it. Most of the entries appear to be her own thoughts, some quotes from various authors. 'Those soft-voiced young men cruel in their carelessness.' 'Optimism – expect the worst of everybody and you won't be disappointed.'

Each entry has a date and two blank lines between the next entry. The first was written seven years ago. 'I trust more in selfish honesty than in unselfish integrity.' 'I detest banter; it sears the soul and deadens the feelings ...' – Honoré de Balzac. 'Might as well ask a politician for a straight answer.' 'All the civilised virtues have been perpetrated by anti-social beings.' 'A happy childhood you take for granted; an unhappy childhood you carry with you through your life.' 'Hunger doesn't own ideals.'

'Prospect, and not possession, was what gave pleasure …' – C S Forrester. 'Beware of praise from your enemies.' That last entry was dated three months previously.

Herbie fingers through the records and CDs below the stereo. Majority are opera. Some choral. A couple of symphonies. No inscriptions on the sleeves. On the corner of one record cover, *La Traviata*, 'With love, Barry.' Her brother is not called Barry.

Herbie returns to the kitchen, pours himself a cup of coffee, takes it with him to the bedroom. The double bed, beneath the multi-coloured heap of clothes, is unmade. The drawers lie, naked chipboard bottoms up, around the bed. Many of the clothes are still folded. Even the knickers.

Herbie looks inside the white bedside cabinets. Two paperbacks. One on faith healing. One on education. A woman's magazine. No diary.

Her jewellery box has been tipped out onto the white dressing table. A chunky necklace, some wooden beads, plastic bangles. No silver. No gold.

Herbie frowns.

He looks again into and behind the bedside cabinets, goes on his hands and knees and looks under the bed. No dust. No watch. Her arms were bare. A radio clock on the floor. He picks up a couple of square perfume bottles, opens and sniffs them. The built-in wardrobe has one fur coat. He searches its pockets. A folded tissue. He makes his way along the hangers looking in other pockets.

The clothes are hung in combinations ready to wear, even to the silk scarf. On the floor of the wardrobe shoes and boots are neatly lined up in pairs. The winter boots have paper stuffed inside them. At the back of the wardrobe is a large empty leather suitcase.

The bathroom is clinically clean. The towels have been taken by forensic. A stiff dry flannel lies over the plastic bath tray. A bar of pink soap in a china dish by the basin, another in the bath tray. In the mirrored cabinet one shelf is half empty. On the other shelves the deodorants, colognes, tampons, ointments, lotions, pills, shampoos are meticulously spaced out. The half-empty shelf is clean, no dust marks, no spill rings to show what was there. He unscrews the top of the cologne bottle, waves it under his nose. Replaces it.

In a locker at the foot of the bath are some clean towels, a woman's electric leg shaver, a hairdryer. In the holder by the basin, one toothbrush. Herbie makes a note of the chemist's address on the label for the pills.

"Sir?" someone calls from the flat doorway.

A detective holds the flat door closed. "Papers are here."

"Let 'em in." Herbie comes down the four steps from the bedroom. Three newspaper men come brushing against one another into the living room.

"Took your time," Herbie says.

"Bigger story. What you got? Rape? Robbery?"

Herbie shakes his head. "Family affair. Boyfriend. Know him?" He holds up the photograph taken in the bar. None of the reporters recognise the man.

"Was it him?" one asks.

"Don't think so. The one who did it cleared the place out. Just a matter now of running him to ground. We got some evidence."

"What?"

"That I can't say. Don't want him to cover his tracks."

"How was she killed?"

"Battered. Messy. By the phone there. With a metal statuette thing. Of a dancer."

"She a dancer?"

"No. I got a photograph of her. We'll get some copies taken, let you have both. If you could ask the man to come forward. Eliminate him from our enquiries."

"That all?"

"She was Katherine Helen Soames. Age twenty-eight. A scientist. Liked opera. One brother. Parents alive. That's about it."

"Rape?"

"They had sex before he killed her."

"Fair enough."

They make to leave. One stops at the door. "Motive?"

"Domestic affair. Lovers' tiff."

The reporter nods, follows his colleagues out.

"Short and sweet." The detective raises his eyebrows.

"Not half." Herbie hands the two photographs to the detective. "You take these back. Run off enough copies for us and the reptiles. If you walk back to the Yard you can slope off afterwards. See you in the morning."

Herbie takes the lift down with the detective, gets out in the dust-sheeted lobby. Trestles and scaffolding lean against the double entrance doors. The caretaker's is signposted off to the side of the lift shaft.

The caretaker's wife opens the door. She is large and fat. Herbie introduces himself. She sighs. "Better come in. He's having his supper."

Furniture in the flat is cheaper than that on the seventh floor. The caretaker is at a thin-legged table in the small kitchen, empty smeared plate before him. The wife returns to the telly in the living room. The caretaker has a round wrinkled face and sparse hair. His hands are small. He doesn't smile.

"Sorry to bother you again. When you've finished eating could you come down and show me which car was Miss Soames's?"

"She didn't have one." He has a cockney accent.

Herbie studies the small caretaker: this man does not like the police. "She paid rent for a parking space."

"Had it for visitors. Complained if anyone else parked there. Always bending me ear about it." This man does not like anyone.

"Ever see any of her visitors' cars parked there?"

"Don't go down there. Unless I have to. Sweep up once a week. Not paid to pry here, you know."

"Did you see much of her? If she didn't have a car she must have used the street entrance."

"Normally, yeah."

"Did you see her?"

"Sometimes."

"Did she get a taxi? Bus? What?"

"Dunno."

"What's her parking space?"

"D8. Behind the lift."

"You ever see her with anyone?"

"Not that I can think of. Quiet tenant. 'Cept for that parking space."

"Did you have to go down and move cars so that her visitors could park there?"

"Can't go moving cars, can I? That's illegal. No." The caretaker thinks. "No. She'd always come to me and say something like 'I had a guest last night who couldn't park his car.' And she'd have the number of the car that was in her place. After that she'd go down and check. Make my life misery until I found out who it was parking their car there, tell 'em not to park there any more."

"But you never saw her visitor's car?"

"Not that I know of. Might've done. But I didn't take any notice. Usually what I looked for was to see if her space was empty. If there was a car there – one I knew shouldn't be there – I'd think 'oh no, here comes trouble.' So I tried not to look. If you know what I mean."

"And you never saw her with anyone?"

"Might've. But there's people in and out of here all day long. Don't keep regular hours, this lot. And her visitors, coming by car, if that's what you're after, well they'd all go up in the lift."

"Thank you. If you do remember anything about her, anything you think might help us, can you let us know?"

"Who d'you reckon did it?"

"The boyfriend who parked his car down there."

The caretaker ponders on that information, then shakes his head. "Like I said, even if he's been coming here for years, if he came up by the lift I wouldn't have seen him."

"Did you see Miss Soames come home today?"

"No. She'd have come in through the carpark, see."

"Where were you between three and six?"

"Half two, thereabouts, I went to pick up the wife. From her sister's in Streatham. I do the cleaning in the mornings. Three floors a day. After I done the rubbish. Afternoons are mine. Unless I'm doing something for one of 'em."

"Where do you keep the rubbish bins?"

"Big ones, you mean? Behind the big louvre doors by the lift shaft. Think he's put stuff in there?"

"He's taken stuff from the flat. Got to have dumped it somewhere. Diary and wristwatch we're looking for. You ever do anything for Miss Soames?"

"Probably did her waste disposal once. They're always going bloody wrong. They overload 'em. And it's a fixture so I got no choice."

"You been in her flat?"

The caretaker scratches with dirty fingernails at the dandruff in his thin hair. "Can't remember for certain. Probably one time or another. Been next door. Where she hides the dog."

"You park your car in the carpark?"

"I'm not supposed to."

"You do?"

"Yeah."

"Where?"

"Wherever there's space. Usually someone's got a space they paid for but forgot about. Or theirs is in the garage. Always somewhere."

"You ever use Miss Soames's place?"

"Once. Once was enough. She threatened to write to The Company."

"When was that?"

"Years ago."

"What if there's no spaces?"

"I squeeze it in the corner. Long as the others can get in and out they don't mind. Doesn't happen often."

"What time did you get back from Streatham?"

"Gone five."

"Did you notice if there was a car in Miss Soames's place?"

"No, because the space I'm using is right opposite the lift entrance. Hers is behind it."

"Did you see anyone down there? In the lift?"

"No. No one. First I knew about it was your blokes asking me to open the barriers."

"Right. Thanks a lot. We'll be here a while yet. We've got to find this visitor who used her parking space. Once we've done that we'll be out of your way."

"Reckon it was him?"

"Won't know for certain until we find him. Can you leave the barriers open for a few days?"

The caretaker pulls a face of exasperation. Habitual response to being asked to do anything, Herbie decides, ignores it.

'How fragile this life is ... how one microbe can steal your sensibility ... make you cough out your existence.'

Barry Popieluszko. The Watcher: Kerala Books.

Monday: 22:56

Herbie sits in one of the squad cars, his feet on the cold carpark floor. His team stand around him. Many of the tenants have not been home.

"Not one I saw," one detective complains, "knew who I was talking about."

"What about 24 and 25," Herbie asks, "and 20 and 21?"

"25 wasn't home." A detective consults his notebook. "24 knew her by sight. But that was all."

"20 and 21 were out all day," another detective says. "Knew her by sight. Keen on privacy, this lot."

"What about over the road?"

"Complete blank."

"We're going to have to come back tomorrow with the photos. I want to know who she was seen with – male or female. And I want two men down here tomorrow morning, stopping everyone who comes in here, asking if they've ever seen anyone parking their car in D8. Behind there. I want 'em here first thing – about six – when people start leaving for work. Use the barriers. Get their names. That includes the milkman and postman. Any other regular visitors to the flats. You two. And I want you to find out who's got the parking bays next to hers. D8, that is. If they can remember the same car being parked there more than once. If they saw its owner. Any car they remember being parked there."

Herbie takes a breath, looks around at the other detectives. "And I want two of you up in the flat all night. Matey boy might be back. Something he might've overlooked. You two weren't on the weekend? Right, I want you to log everyone who gets out of the lift on that floor. Or anyone who goes by on the stairs. You can use the kitchen to make coffee, but I want someone on the stairs all night. Up to you when you two relieve them at six. One of you dodge up there now, get a Polaroid of the painting above the stereo. Lilies. Take a couple. And during the night one of you can go through the rubbish bins. Behind the louvre doors there." A few of the other detectives grin. "We're looking for a package containing a diary and a wristwatch. Maybe some other stuff. A couple of records, possibly. I've notified the banks about the credit cards. That's it. The rest of you meet me in the morning. No point in getting people out of bed this time of night. We're all tired. He thinks he's covered his tracks. He's not going anywhere he's not already got. Tell the uniforms they can go. Now," Herbie wearily stands, "once I've got that photo I'll follow you back, make out my report. Let's all try and get a reasonably early night. Eh?"

Tuesday: 09:08

The big room feels like a horizontal slice of the tall building, its desks and bright windows divided by noticeboards on castors. Plastic coffee cups lie among the telephones and wordprocessors on the desktops. Herbie's team occupy their corner. Only a few of the other desks and chairs are being used.

"What you reckon?" Jim asks Herbie.

"On what?"

"This."

One of the detectives holds up a newspaper. The front page contains only the headline 'SIX DAYS TO END OF WORLD.'

"What about it?" Herbie asks Jim.

"You believe it? It's in all the papers. On telly last night. Nothing else but, this morning."

"Time I did my report, got home last night, Sal was in bed. She said something. Thought she was dreaming."

Some of his detectives laugh. Laugh laughs.

"Saw it stuck up outside newsagents when I come in," Herbie says. "Thought it was some gimmick. What, they reckon it's true?"

"All over. Russians reckon it's going to come earlier."

"Six days?"

"That's what the Yanks reckon."

"Why?"

"The universe is contracting."

"Say we got to go out and look at the stars tonight," a detective says from behind his paper. "Got star charts and everything here."

"What we supposed to see?"

"More stars. Stars that weren't there before."

"It's a con." Herbie dismisses it. "When did you lot last look at the stars?"

By their lack of response the other detectives make known their disagreement with him.

"Miss Soames get a mention?"

"Nothing but this in the papers."

"No sport?"

"A few results. That's all."

"You lot believe it?"

Herbie is answered with shrugs.

"What's it say we're supposed to do?"

"Doesn't say."

"Nothing?"

"Says we're powerless."

"Hold on. Get some sense on this." Herbie has picked up a phone, dials. "Mike? Herbie. What's the word on all this is the papers?"

"End of the world stuff, you mean?"

"Yeah."

"Only wish I knew."

"So what do we do?"

"Dunno. Carry on as normal until told otherwise, I suppose."

"That's it?"

"That's it. You'd better concentrate on Katherine Helen Soames. Let the stake-out ride. Nothing'll happen there until

Friday anyway. I got no one to spare so you'll have to manage with what you got."

"Can I cancel the stake-out?"

"Better not."

"Thanks."

"It's got to be true," one of the detectives is low-voiced saying. "They couldn't pull a stunt like this if it wasn't. Look at the mischief it'll cause. Got to be true."

"The word is we carry on as normal until told otherwise," Herbie says.

"What's the point?" the detective says. "If it's all going to come to a full stop in six days?"

"And what if it doesn't?"

The detectives are silent.

"But what if it does?" Jim says. "End, I mean."

"How can they be so sure it's six days?" Herbie asks them. "Look, it took millions and millions of years for the universe to get this big. Suddenly it's all going to be over in six days? Do me a favour."

"No," the detective who has been arguing its truth says, "this has already been happening for millions of years. But, because it's been happening at the extremes of the universe, it's only been noticed in the last couple of years. It takes millions of years for their light to reach us."

"So how's the world going to end?"

"Because the universe was expanding. Now it's all coming back. And we're slap bang in the way of it all."

"If it took millions of years for the light from those stars to reach us, then it stands to reason it's going to take as long for the stars themselves to reach us."

"No. Because they're now travelling faster than the speed of light. And apparently as they collide with other stars they accelerate."

"OK," Herbie says. "If this has been happening for millions of years, how come it's only six days?"

"Up until last week," the detective searches rustling through his paper, "they thought it was going to be billions of years. Some of them didn't even believe that the universe was contracting. Then last week they found loads more new stars. They'd underestimated its speed."

"There you go then," Herbie says. "What's it say in there about those who don't believe the universe is contracting?"

"They think," he quotes, "it's a load of dangerous rubbish."

"I'll go along with that. And in seven days' time so will everybody else. What exactly do they reckon will happen on this sixth day? Just how, precisely, will it all end?"

"They say we won't know what hit us. The stuff coming at us is moving so fast, millions of times the speed of light, they say, we won't even have time to blink."

"Says here," another detective says, "if it happens at night we'll be able to see the first bits and pieces burning up in the atmosphere. 'A fireworks night to end all fireworks nights.'"

"You mean they don't even know if it'll be day or night? Yet they're rock solid certain it's going to be in exactly six days?"

"They say here it'll hit us before the sun. But if it was winter and it did hit the sun first we might have just one second's warning. That's how fast it's going."

"Supposed to be going," Herbie says. "In six days time they'll all be explaining why they were so mistaken. In the meantime we carry on as normal until told otherwise. You get anything on those painters, Jim?"

The debate is over: it is back to business. The detectives shift their posture.

"Clean," Jim says. "All of 'em. Saw nothing."

"Larceny? Nothing?"

·"Their boss checks them out. Got to be left on their tod in people's houses."

"What about the PM?"

"Nothing new." Jim looks down the report, reads bits, "Time of death 4:10. Primary cause of death – cerebral haemorrhage, busted brain. Assailant's blood group – from sperm – O positive."

"Great," Herbie says. "He's sure the assailant is the one who had sex with her?"

Jim flicks through the pages of the report. "Doesn't say. The assumption is made."

"Forensic?"

"Nothing on the prints." Jim changes reports. "They reckon no one, save for victim and assailant, and Mrs Harris next door, was in flat. Spittle on fag ends also blood group O positive. Suit material – from towel – summer lightweight. Residual dust – some dog's hairs. Next door's. London street dirt. Fag ash. Hair on pillow grey. Recently cut. No dyes, no setting lotion. Eyebrows black. Pubic hairs black. Skin tissue pigmentation – white. Age from chromosome count, somewhere between forty and fifty."

"Sugar daddy?" one detective says.

"Don't look !ike it: she earned good money," Herbie tells him. "Night shift reported in?"

"No one came near the flat last night. Nothing in the bins."

Herbie nods, arranges the papers Jim has given him on his desk. "We're looking for a boyfriend. A regular boyfriend. He tried to remove anything that could link him to her. Motive? – lover's tiff, got out of hand. Wasn't premeditated. He just tried to clear out as fast as he could after. Her brother's called Ben. One record was given to her by someone called Barry. We got this one photograph of her with a man. We do have it?" Herbie looks around at his team. He is handed two envelopes.

Removing enlargements of the studio portrait and the one of her in the bar with a man, he pins them both onto a noticeboard.

"Is he the one?" a detective asks.

"Not unless," Herbie returns to his desk, "he's gone prematurely grey. But he might be able to tell us who her current boyfriend is. Whoever the boyfriend was he cleared out any photos of himself. If there were any. The only possible witness we've got at the moment is a deaf goldminer's widow." A few of the detectives respond to this, as he intended, with smiles. "But we do," Herbie emphasises, "have his prints and a few odds and ends he might've overlooked. Someone bought a painting for her from this address." He shows his notebook to Jim. Jim starts copying the address. "I want you to check that out," he tells Jim, "see who bought it. Polaroids here. And I want you to organise a rota in the carpark. Show the photos about, see if you can trace the car that parked in D8. With a bit of luck someone may have had a bump or scrape with it. You can take the two off the flat, put a seal on it. The rest of you go on the knocker. Show the photos. Ask if she was ever seen with a man. Any man. Knock up even those you went to yesterday." Herbie looks frowning around the office. "We seem short."

"Lee and Sanders both called in sick."

"Did they?" A team leader's sarcasm, not a question.

Herbie turns a page of his notebook. "I want someone sympathetic to go and see the brother. You. Southampton address." He hands his notebook to the detective. "She got letters from him regularly. So you can suppose she wrote to him. Any man she mentioned at all. The letters if he's kept them. Or any idea he might have who did it. You can bring him up to officially identify her."

"Thanks, pal."

"Mind going on your own? Only we're short all round today. Same for everyone."

The detective gives a shake of his head.

"You'd better get going." Herbie consults his notebook. "And I want you," he nods to another detective, "to find out who her doctor was, see if you can find out why she was on these pills. Nothing in the PM on that?" he asks Jim. "Pregnant or anything?"

"Nothing."

"And then check with the chemist, see if they can remember who collected the prescription. And you," he selects another detective, "can check out the suit material. With a bit of luck it might've been a small batch. Find out which tailors got it, a list of the people they made suits for. I can't see matey buying off the peg." Herbie turns back the pages of his notebook. "OK. That's it."

"What about you?" Jim asks him.

"I'm off to Chiswick. See the people she worked with. Meet you back here."

"What I don't get," Jim says, "is why he left the door open for the dog to run in there?"

"His one oversight?"

"If he hadn't we mightn't have found her for days. Maybe never now."

Tuesday: 10:43

The Managing Director of CAS Ltd is black, bald, tall and thin, his face deeply grooved, eyes nicotine red.

The office is a working shambles. Designs of machinery are pinned one atop the other to sloping draughtsman's boards, computers and VDUs have piles of printout upon them and beside them; and on the desk is heaped more paper, with stacks of it slewed around the floor.

Mr Trellpott picks his way with the ease of long practice through the litter, advances on Herbie hand outstretched. As their hands touch he says his name, "Trellpott," and blinks. Formality is this man's everyday defence.

Releasing the narrow hand, Herbie gives his own title and surname.

"And what can I do for you, Inspector?"

"It concerns one of your employees."

"Which one would that be?"

"Katherine Helen Soames."

"Kate?"

"She was murdered yesterday afternoon."

"Murdered?"

Mr Trellpott stares at Herbie, looks around the room, back to Herbie. "Murdered?"

"Where were you yesterday afternoon?"

"Me? Here. Well, not here, down in the workshop."

"What time did you leave?"

"Leave?" Mr Trellpott is looking through Herbie, his mind busy with images, calculations, considerations. He focuses on Herbie, remembers. "Me leave here? Must have been gone nine."

"Were you on your own?"

"After six I was. Look … Yes, I remember, she got a call yesterday. Somebody looking for her. I'm sorry," he reaches out long knobbly fingers to Herbie. "I've got to sit down."

Mr Trellpott trips over a stack of papers, stumbles to a high office chair, holds onto a draughtsman's board. He shakes his head. "Kate murdered …"

Herbie has seen culprits act shock: it looked like this.

"She got a call yesterday?" he persists. "That so unusual?"

"She was out on site. They insisted on being connected with her. She didn't have her mobile. We've been having trouble with the company. I had to come up here to find the number. It's a new factory." Mr Trellpott flicks his free hand in the air as he talks. The other hand continues to support him.

"Man or woman caller?"

"I've no idea. I can ask the switchboard."

"You didn't speak directly to them?"

"No. No reason."

"And she left the site?"

"Where was she murdered? Kate murdered," he tells himself.

"In her flat."

"In the afternoon? Yes of course the afternoon."

"Did you know she'd left the site?"

"No. Never gave it another thought. No reason to."

"Was she due on site this morning?"

"No, she'd have come here first. We have a production meeting every morning. Well, nothing so formal – a get-together over coffee when we first come in."

"Didn't you wonder why she didn't turn up this morning?"

"No. Not this morning."

"Why not?"

"Come on … You not heard the news?"

"You believe all that?"

Mr Trellpott shrugs, glances nervously down about his desk. "Most of my staff do. None of them turned in today."

"Who were all of those people downstairs, then?"

"I meant my executive staff. Give the receptionists another day and they'll believe it too."

"What was Katherine Soames's position here?"

"Was? She's our Project Manager. Installation and follow-through."

"Installing what?"

"Robots. Customised robots. Kate's job is to assess the customer's needs, see how best we can meet that need. That means she's often out on site. You see, you can get an all-purpose robot, but then you've got a load of functions you've paid for going to waste. We streamline the process, provide for specific needs. One-offs."

"Would you have been surprised that Kate went home early yesterday? Would it have been that unusual?"

"No, not really. We more or less keep to office hours, but we have deadlines to meet. So sometimes it means working late. Or over the weekends. My staff know what's to be done. I have to trust their judgement. They know if they can give themselves an afternoon off."

"Was Kate ill earlier this year?"

Mr Trellpott ponders that. "Yes. Yes she was. Septicemia. Cut herself on a tin, or something. Her arm was swollen. Took a week off. But there again, you see, she didn't really have a week off. Liz took her work around for her. We were rushed. Kate carried on by phone."

"Liz?"

"Liz Bradley. Head of our research team here." He pauses. "Liz is our research team."

"She in today?"

"No. Not today."

"How long has Kate worked here?"

"About five, no six years. She came straight here from college. PhD."

"Have you been to her flat?"

"Couple of times. Like when she was ill. And I went there once for a dinner party. Someone was leaving."

"Did you ever wonder how she could afford such an expensive apartment?"

"She had no other commitments. As far as I know. And she made good money here."

"She ever mention any boyfriends?"

"Not so far as I know. She isn't, wasn't, that kind of girl. Didn't gossip at all. She may have told Liz, though. They used to meet outside work. How did she die?"

"Battered to death."

"In her flat?"

"Yes. What kind of car do you drive?"

"That flat was always so neat. Though I suppose she'd have tidied it beforehand. Before I went round. No," he wags a long finger at Herbie, "she didn't know I was coming when I popped in with the files. Was it a robbery? Did she disturb a burglar?"

"What makes you ask that?"

"That's what usually happens. Isn't it?"

"Her assailant was known to her. What kind of car do you drive?"

"A Fiat. She knew him?"

"What colour?"

"It's yellow. A vile yellow."

"Why keep it if you don't like the colour?"

"Easy to find in carparks," he says, accompanied by his usual laugh whenever he says it. He hears his own laugh, asks, "Was she badly marked?"

"She was beaten to death. Do you have Liz Bradley's address?"

"Not here. Wages'll have it."

"Did Kate keep a diary?"

"Must have. Yes, she must have."

"Can I look through her office?"

"Yes of course. It's three doors along. On the left."

Herbie moves to leave, pauses. "How many of your executive staff did turn in this morning?"

"I did."

"Were you surprised?"

"Not really. It's been the main topic of debate here for months. Practically all of us have science degrees, read scientific papers. It's been speculated on for practically a year. Now there appears to be no doubt."

"You believe it, then?"

"Looks like it."

"So why bother coming to work?"

Mr Trellpott picks up a piece of metal from beside the draughtsman's board, turns it over in his hands. "I don't honestly know." He smiles at Herbie. "Habit, I suppose. And what about you? Seems a bit pointless trying to find one murderer when we're all about to die."

"What if we don't?"

"I think that's part of my reckoning too. What if next week comes and we're all still here? What if we're all here for another

47

year? What are we going to do in the meantime? We can hardly sit round waiting for it to happen."

"Do you recognise this man?" Herbie shows him the photograph.

"Sorry." Mr Trellpott looks around for his glasses, can't find them, squints at the photograph. "No. Sorry. Looks like any number of people. Kate had her hair like that when she first came here."

"Thank you, Mr Trellpott. You've been most helpful."

"I'm going to phone Liz in a minute." Mr Trellpott stands. "Find out what everyone's doing. I might close for a week. I don't know. Not sure what to do. Is it all right if I tell Liz about Kate? Tell her that you're coming to see her?"

"Can you ask her to stay in? Would she be likely to?"

"Liz would. Yes, Liz would."

"If you have to, then tell her. And thank you Mr Trellpott."

The names are on the office doors. L Bradley's office is next to K Soames. Katherine Soames's office is the same size as Mr Trellpott's; but where Mr Trellpott's appeared a disorganised jumble, Katherine Soames's is a picture of orderliness, seems therefore to be larger.

Here too are designs clipped to sloping draughtsman's boards, and a computer. But nowhere here is there a loose stack of papers. The drawers all have labels on them. On the windowsill is a large potted fern. The desk top is clear save for keyboard, printer, VDU and a pen holder. On the wall beside the desk is a large calendar. Some dates are neatly bracketed. Contract completion dates, Herbie guesses.

Sitting behind the desk he opens the top left hand drawer. A box of tissues, some loose tampons, a few cosmetics. In the right hand drawer some draughtsman's pens, a calculator, rulers, protractors, Tippex, ink, sellotape, scissors, staples.

In the middle drawer two files, her handwriting on their covers. In the lower drawers more files.

Herbie shuts the drawers, looks around the office. She had expected to return here. A life rudely interrupted. An organised life in full spate. But no diary.

Tuesday: 11:53

Herbie sits in his car in the carpark of CAS Ltd, his phone in his hand. "Jim? How'd you get on with the picture?"

"Blank. The bloke who owns the shop's away on a buying trip. His wife only helps out in the shop on the odd occasion. He called last night from somewhere in Wales. Can't pronounce it. He's not there anymore anyway. All being well he's due back day after tomorrow."

"Fair enough. Can you go to Bethnal Green now? A new factory in Warner Place. Boysons. She was there yesterday installing some robots. A man phoned her here, was given their number. He didn't leave his name here. After she got the call she went home. See if anyone there overheard the telephone conversation. Any names mentioned. Find out exactly what time she left. And you better check out the movements of everybody who was there yesterday. Run 'em through records."

"Where will you be?"

"Clapham. Her work friend. Then I'll probably stop off in Victoria. See you back in the office."

'It's not our disparate individuality which astonishes, nor our uniqueness, nor our grey similarity; rather it's the way it all meshes.'
Barry Popieluszko. Psychotic Android Eats: Fire Dragon.

Tuesday: 13:27

The flat is the basement of a large house opposite Clapham Common. Herbie parks his car in the gravel forecourt. Going down the steps to the flat he burps up his sausage and chips cafe lunch. (He suffers the indigestion and heartburn of shift workers.)

Hanging outside the flat's maroon door is an old ship's bell. Herbie swings it. It is noisy in his ear.

Through the frosted glass of the door he sees a woman in white with fierce red hair. The door opens.

Liz Bradley has on a long white towelling robe. In her early thirties, she has dark lines under her eyes, a sullen mouth.

Herbie holds open his ID. "Detective Inspector Watkins. Miss Bradley? Did Mr Trellpott call you?"

"It's Mrs Bradley. And yes, he did." She steps back from the door. "Come in."

A long narrow hall faces him. She and the flat smell of fag smoke. Herbie goes through the first open door into a gloomy room. Painted a deep red, it is crowded with potted plants and is close with the iron-soapy breath of a menstruating woman.

The one window has slatted blinds. Opposite the window is a long and deep maroon sofa.

"Not that the Mrs means anything." Liz Bradley follows him into the room. "Mr walked out on me last week."

"I'm sorry."

"I'm not. Like a coffee?"

"If it's no trouble."

Herbie follows her along the hall to the kitchen. White and bright, it is crowded with cupboards, has no room for chairs.

"I've been trying to feel sorry for Kate." She holds the kettle under the tap. "I've been trying to feel angry about it. But I can't." She plugs in the kettle. "No sense of personal loss, I suppose. Doubt that I'd have seen her again anyway before the week's out. She's just gone a few days ahead of the rest of us."

"It was a brutal murder," Herbie tells her. "She had her arm broken trying to defend herself."

"Even so …" She takes down two patterned mugs from a cupboard. "Even so, I don't see the point of your investigation. Even if you catch him in time he'll never have his day in court. So what if you catch him today? He'll spend a couple of days in jail, then go with the rest of us." She spoons instant coffee into the mugs. "Sugar?"

"One, please."

"Ask yourself what's the point of catching him. To deter others. What others? Haven't you got anything better to do with your last few days?"

"You believe all this end of the world stuff, then?"

"Don't take my word for it. Take a look at the stars tonight."

"I wouldn't know what I was looking for."

"No need. There'll be a lot more stars there than you've ever seen before."

"Always seemed a lot to me."

"You are a sceptical man."

The kettle is boiling.

"Must be my job." He pulls a mock-rueful face. "People tell me lies every day."

She smiles for the first time at him. "Milk?"

"Please."

Handing him his coffee, she makes to move past him. Herbie steps aside, gestures her ahead of him.

"Did Kate believe this end of the world stuff?" he asks as they reach the red living room.

"Oh yes," she says. "Once you've seen the facts there's no doubting it."

"What facts?"

"Over the past two years we've seen the universe stop expanding." She puts her coffee mug on the floor, arranges herself in a corner of the sofa. "That's why there are so many more stars. Previously they were going from us so much faster than the speed of light they were undetectable. When they stopped their light became visible."

"I've heard all this already." Herbie lowers himself into a creaking wicker chair opposite the sofa, his back to the window.

Liz Bradley picks up her cigarettes from the floor, lights one. She blows out the smoke, tucks the white towelling robe around her thin ankles. "Do you know why the news broke?" she asks him.

"No."

"Up until last week the only disagreements, real disagreements, were about how many hundreds of years it would be before the end of the world. Then, over a period of six weeks, we watched two galaxies move together and merge into one. Do you know the minimum distance between galaxies? Two million light years. And it took only six weeks for them to collide. And that happened millions of years ago. The astronomers extrapolated those figures, did a few quick sums and came up with ten days for it to reach us.

Four days for the authorities to decide what to do with such hot news. And now you know. You still sceptical?"

"I'm sorry," Herbie shakes his head, "but it all smacks a bit of 'The End Of The World Is Nigh'."

"End of the world? They weren't ambitious enough. It's the end of the frigging universe."

"And Kate believed all this?"

"Yes," she says, sinks back into the gloom of the room.

"What was Kate's attitude to it?"

"Same as mine. Anger. Futility." She rolls her head on the back of the sofa, stops and studies him. "You still don't realise what it means, do you?"

"I only heard this morning."

"Of course." She closes her eyes. "I'm sorry. I've had so much longer to think about it. And it caused me sleepless nights when the prognosis came down to hundreds of years. You see," she opens her eyes, looks directly at him, "it means the end of everything. We're powerless to overcome it. It's not like the old prediction for the end of the world -- under what we'd come to think of as the natural order. That was a slow end. The sun dying, the earth gradually becoming uninhabitable. Incapable of sustaining life anyway. And that was five thousand million years hence. By then we could have moved to other planets. To other solar systems. We had a foreseeable future. Of sorts. We had hope. Now – nothing."

"What's caused it?"

"You can take your pick of several theories. The one I favour is that it's a perpetual process. The universe began with a bang, bits shot off in all directions. Those bits became stars, planets, galaxies, etcetera. We thought we were on the edge of that expanding universe. We were not. It's much bigger than we thought. Only now it's getting smaller by the second; because, having reached its limit, it has rapidly begun to contract, will compact into one huge star. The force of that impact will cause it to explode. And the whole process will start over again. Galaxies will form. Stellar systems will be formed. Life will evolve. Then the universe will again reach its limits, will once more start to contract, and wipe out all life. All life. All memory of life."

"Why hasn't it just carried on expanding?"

"That no one knows. Must reach a quantum state of sorts. Some reckon it's a law of thermodynamics. To do with loss of sustainable heat caused by the expansion. Some believe it's due to a now unproveable law of gravity. Of mass. Does it matter?"

Her mouth is set in misery.

"This why your husband left you?"

"My dear husband took a hard look at what little future was left him, and decided that he didn't want to spend it with me." She grinds out her cigarette. She has smoked it down to the filter. "It was mutual," she says, quieter now. "I'm not sure yet that you realise how much the idea of a future governs our lives. All our lives. All of our lives. With no future I suddenly realised that I didn't have to have sex with him if I didn't want to. I've never much enjoyed it with him. And there was no longer any other reason for sex. To please him, to have babies, to secure my marriage – all void. I did in the past – to keep him. But suddenly I didn't have to look attractive any more, I didn't even have to be polite. Why bother? What for? So he left me. So what?"

"Any idea where he's gone?"

"No. And I don't care. Doubt that he does either. Because this hit him as hard. He's an archaeologist. And without a future there is no past. The only point in finding out about the past is for the sake of the future. We can learn from history. But to what end? Without a future those lessons can't be put to use. Even if any discovery he made was of no immediate apparent use, it was still knowledge for knowledge's sake, still added to the sum total of human knowledge, might one day have been of some use ... In five days' time all humanity will be gone forever."

"And Kate thought like this?"

"Of course. We're both trained scientists. Our vision is fixed firmly on the future. On some time hence. So what if we only worked with industrial robots: we made some exciting innovations. To what end now, though? Progress? Progress towards what? Before this I never realised quite how dedicated I was. How much that dedication was assumed in others. We very few of us did it for personal gain. Egotism possibly; but even that assumed a future to be famous in. Until now I never realised how much a part I was of civilisation. That to each of us civilisation itself is a monument to our having been Was a monument. Now when I die all dies. That's the horror of it."

She has paused reflectively. Herbie leaps in, "Did you see Kate yesterday?"

"In the morning. Then she was out on site. Look ..."

"She say anything? Act any differently?"

"No. Look, the real horror of it is that all our chances have gone. If we'd got into space just a hundred years sooner then maybe we could've beaten it, have still been here for when it started over again. How many times d'you reckon intelligent beings have got as far as us only to be wiped out?"

"So humankind could come again?"

"Some intelligence might. Though not necessarily. Might not even be enough time for life to evolve next time. This could have been our one big chance. And we blew it."

"Would Kate have gone to work today?"

Liz Bradley ignores the question, drinks her coffee. "I suppose we would have said that we liked our jobs because they were interesting. Would have sounded ridiculous to us if anyone had said we were working to improve the lot of the whole of humanity. But we were. Now there will be no humanity. Now there is no point any more in working. Because scientists see beyond their own individual deaths. Even the lowliest of us. Despite our death our work might have been of some use. Might have added to the sum of human wisdom. In the future. It all takes for granted a continuation. A survival of the species. Which is why I was opposed to nuclear power. So that we wouldn't wipe out our species. So that there would be a future. Otherwise what was the point? And it was a debt I owed to past scientists. To build upon their work. So I had to try to stop nuclear proliferation or all their efforts would have been wasted. It was for the sake of humanity. Big words again. But that's what it comes down to when you look closely at it. It's only now, when you step back, that you see how immense it is. In time. How long it took us to reach here." She sighs, deflated. "Ironical, eh? There we've been worried for decades about blowing ourselves up. Now we're having it done for us."

Herbie moves to speak. She forestalls him, "Do you realise now the absolute hopelessness of it? Of your job too? Ask yourself why are there policemen? Ask yourself why the catching of one criminal is so important? It's for the sake of the future. So that this society will not descend into chaos. In five days' time there'll be no society. No one to impress with the catching of your one murderer. So what's the point?"

Herbie gazes down into his mug, at the remaining coffee. He drinks it.

"I was talking to a doctor last week," she says. "He's on the same nuclear committee. Now a doctor has to be a social being. If the person he cures this week is run over the next, is slaughtered in a war, what's the point of his expertise? Now this doctor is about to lose all his patients for evermore. But he's going to go on working. Know why? He said he can dish out sedatives beforehand. He at least is looking at the only future we've got. You see, we have all of us been trained to think of the future. To consider consequences. The idea of the future has justified all morality, all law, all action. Being cruel to be kind assumes a future. In five days' time there's no tomorrow. So what are you doing it for?"

Herbie sits silent and apparently glum. "At the moment," Herbie brings his head up, "I don't know what else to do. And I don't want him just to go with the rest of us. When he killed her he thought he had a future. The law still applies to him." He makes a helpless gesture. "That's why I'm a policeman."

She, frowning, studies him, reaches down to the floor for her cigarettes. "You've listened to my maudlin ramblings," she smiles maternally on him, "so how can I help you?"

Herbie returns the smile. "Thank you." He takes out his notebook. "You were a close friend of Kate's?"

"No." She shakes her head. "Kate isn't, wasn't, the kind of woman who had close friends."

"But you did meet her outside of work?"

"We shared a love of opera. Had season tickets to Covent Garden. We spent two weeks in Bayreuth one year. Last year we did Italy. La Scala."

"You were married then?"

"He was away on a dig. It wasn't much of a marriage."

"Have you been to Kate's flat?"

"A few times. Called in for coffee after an evening out."

"You ever meet anyone there?"

"A man, you mean? No. A dinner party once. But it was all work people. Wives. Husbands."

"Who partnered Kate?"

"No one. An old college friend was there. A girl."

"Remember her name?"

"Sorry."

"Did Kate keep a diary?"

"No idea."

"I mean did you ever see her with a diary? Appointment diary?"

"Yes. Always had her organiser in her hand at morning meetings. Not a big one. Usual size. Is it missing?"

Herbie nods. "Did she ever make any mention at all of men friends to you?"

"Kate wasn't that kind of woman. It's all in neat little compartments. Stone-walled compartments. I used to think it odd that with her own life so neatly portioned up she should be our overall coordinator. Then I came to see that it wasn't that odd. She was used to making all her own little compartments present a unified whole. The same with us in all our little offices."

"You never once saw her with a man?"

"Not once. I assumed though that there had to be a man somewhere in the background. She couldn't make certain dates, never gave a reason. Though that's later. The last few years. When she first started at CAS I think she was living with someone Camden way. North London, anyway. I remember when she moved she was looking for furniture, wanted a sofa like this one."

"She ever bring anyone here?"

"No."

"What makes you think there was a man in the background, then?"

"Nothing specific. She knew what I was talking about when I was grousing about my husband. And opera. Had to be either a Friday or a Saturday evening. She was always busy the rest of the week."

"Same with holidays?"

"No. Oddly enough. She just fitted her dates in with mine. I admired her, you know. She was a very independent lady. Without making a big fuss about it."

"What did you talk about with her?"

"This. That. Work. People. Whatever was in the news. Matters of the moment. Can't remember exactly. I may have done most of the talking. No," she stubs out her cigarette, "I don't think so."

"Does Mr Trellpott smoke? Only I didn't notice any cigarettes there, forgot to ask."

"I'm the only one at CAS who smokes. A nicotine leper."

"What about your husband?"

"No. Smugly self-righteous about it too. We didn't have much in common."

"Was Kate a member of your nuclear group?"

"Dunno. If she wasn't she was a sympathiser."

"You any idea who might've killed her?"

"None. None whatsoever. Was it someone who knew her?"

"Regular visitor to her flat. She ever mention her family to you?"

"Maybe. In passing. She went home to her parents some weekends."

"That all?"

"Do you know, before today I would have said that I knew Kate moderately well. I now realise quite how little I do know about her. But you know how it is – some people tell you their life story ten minutes after you've met them. About their sex life, their hysterectomies. There's a telephonist at CAS like it. I heard her on the phone once telling it all to a complete stranger. Just a voice. Then you've got those like Kate. Trellpott too. You know them for years, or you think you do, and then you accidentally find out something about them and you realise they're complete strangers. Sorry, Inspector."

"Why would she keep her boyfriend secret?"

"Married man, maybe. I don't know. But Kate was like that. She never talked about herself at all. About her past. Nothing. For instance if she'd been me today she'd have opened the door and either answered your questions or not. She wouldn't have mentioned a husband going off, still less the reasons for it. I doubt that she would have even mentioned the end of the universe. She was like that. A wall separating every aspect of her life. Everything was to the point. Very brusque. She could seem rude at times."

"Did she meet any men on your holidays together?"

"No. Wasn't interested. I had a fling in Bayreuth. Opera groupie meets man from chorus. Kate knew about it, never once mentioned it. So far as she was concerned that was my business. Makes her sound prim. She wasn't. It was just that what I did was my own affair. In all senses." She smiles. "I haven't been much help, have I?"

"She did keep a diary?"

"About this big." She holds her hands about twelve centimetres apart. The nails are bitten down. "Always had it on her. She was often out on site."

"Did Kate have a watch?"

"Small gold one, I think. Nothing spectacular. Told the time."

"Do you recognise this man?" Herbie hands her the photograph.

"No." She peers closely at it. "But I guess that'd be Mr Camden. It couldn't have been him?"

"He doesn't fit the one description we have of her regular visitor. Although we'd still like to contact him. Know him?"

She shakes her head, asks, "What does he look like? Her regular visitor?"

"Middle-aged businessman. Greying."

She pulls a face, mouth pursed. Shakes her head, "Sorry. You still going ahead with this then?"

"Why not?"

"Why not indeed."

"Do you drive?"

"Why?"

"Elimination. What kind of car?"

"Saab."

"Colour?"

"Off-white."

"Didn't see it parked up there."

"My husband took it."

Herbie closes his notebook, gets to his feet. "Thanks for all your help, Miss …"

"Liz."

"Liz. And thanks for explaining this universe business. Will you be here if I need to contact you again?"

"I don't know." She reaches for another cigarette. "I have no plans."

'Only by its failures does science advance.'

Barry Popieluszko. The Watcher: Kerala Books.

Tuesday: 16:49

Jim is seated on one of the swivel chairs playing with the keyboard. The detective who went to Southampton is sitting with his feet up on another of the desks.

"Anything?" Herbie greets Jim.

"Blanks all round," Jim says. "Like looking for the invisible man in his invisible car."

"Nothing from the flats?"

"They found the two with the parking bays next to hers. One says the car he most often noticed parked there was a red Rover. The other swears it was a silver-grey BMW. We checked back. Both are absolutely, unshakably, certain."

"No one seen entering or leaving?"

"She had one pint of milk a day. Silver top. Rarely had extra. All letters and parcels delivered addressed to her. So far as the postman can remember. Total bloody blank."

"Nobody on the stairs last night?"

"Only Mrs Harris. Hides her dog under her coat."

"Not easy with a Great Dane." The other detective likes to think of himself as the jester of the team.

"And that's it?" Herbie asks Jim.

"That's it. Sum bloody total."

Herbie drops onto the chair behind his desk. "She's been living in those flats for the last four years, and I reckon he's been visiting her there for as long. But no one, not one tenant, remembers seeing her with anyone. Except Mrs Harris. And it wasn't him." Herbie dismissively indicates the bar photograph on the noticeboard. "What about Bethnal Green?"

"Blank. Except one of the fitters did time for taking and driving away. Prints don't match. And that's it. The phone there is in an empty office. She closed the door while she talked. Said that something had come up, she had to go, would call in the morning. Call came just before one. They were about to go to lunch. Plummy voice. Male. No name. According to the manager."

"How'd she leave? Taxi?"

"She went out before them."

"Bloody marvellous. What about the brother?" Herbie asks the other detective. "He identify her OK?"

"Oh yes. He was sick. Everywhere. And he didn't know she was dead until I breezed in. Thanks very much. I put him on the train to Newbury. To his parents. He's unemployed. You owe me the Newbury fare."

"What'd he tell you? Boyfriend?"

"Hardly knew a thing about her. Didn't even know she was on the phone. I've checked – ex-directory."

"What about her letters to him?"

"Never kept them. He thought, assumed, there was a boyfriend. Didn't think it was any of his business. He was more concerned with this end of the world stuff."

"Ain't they all." Jim stands and stretches.

"He went on and on," the detective says, "like he was some nutty astrologist. 'Know it's true. I seen it in the stars. Hanging there,' he said, 'like luminous mushrooms.' I really am most grateful to you for having had the pleasure of his company."

"Ironical, eh?" Jim taps the noticeboard, "If he'd waited six more days he could've saved himself the trouble."

"Who was seeing the doctor?" Herbie asks him.

"Must've made him ill." Jim picks up a piece of scribbled paper. "He got the squits. Dropped this off on his way home."

"Doctors have that effect on me," the detective says. "Always feel ill after I've seen one."

"The doctor cooperate?"

"Said she was a healthy young woman." Jim deciphers the writing, "Had septicemia earlier this year."

"That the scar on the wrist?"

"Doesn't say."

"No mention of a suicide attempt from anybody? From her brother?"

"None. Not a hint of it. He seemed amazed that she, of all people, would get herself murdered."

"What about the doctor? No abortions? Clap?"

"Was asked, was told not. A standing prescription for oral contraceptives."

"The chemist?"

"So far as he can remember," Jim peers closely at the writing, "the young lady herself collected the prescription. But he wouldn't swear to it."

"Suit material?"

"He was in just now." Jim lays down the sheet of paper. "He's traced it to the suppliers, got a list of the forty-six bespoke tailors who took delivery of it. All over the country. Even Scotland. He's starting with the eleven London tailors. Has seen three so far, is going to call by a couple more on his way home."

"Oh, bloody marvellous." Herbie crushes a plastic coffee cup, crackling it in his fist. "Spoke too bloody soon, didn't I? Be over by Friday." He throws the split coffee cup like a shuttlecock at a wastepaper bin by Jim. Misses. "Fat bloody chance now."

'... the young look for reasons to make life worth living.'
Barry Popieluszko. Raw As Birth: White Swan.

Tuesday: 18:56

The terrace house is in Walworth.

From the tiled hall Herbie can hear the television in the living room. He pushes open the living room door.

Sal is in a black armchair, her stockinged feet up on a suede pouffe. Sal greets the world expressionlessly, her white face a shield. She and Herbie have been married for twenty-two years. Herbie bends to kiss the top of her head. Her black hair is cut short and curled.

"What's for dinner?" Herbie undoes his jacket, lowers himself into the other armchair.

"Salad. Cold chicken."

Sal stiffly swings her feet off the pouffe, sits forward and, bending her legs under her, pushes her feet into her red slippers. "I didn't know how busy you'd be. And I know you didn't eat yesterday."

Sal is the manageress of a works canteen, starts at seven, finishes at three. She left for work just as Herbie was waking this morning: he hasn't phoned today.

The television still holds her attention. She hasn't yet risen from her chair.

"This a video?" Herbie asks.

"Nothing else on. Same as last night. Everybody going on and on about this end of the world stuff." She faces him, "Do you believe it?"

Herbie looks away to the television. He has seen the film at least twice before. "Met some scientists today who had no doubts about it."

Sal abruptly rises. "You want it in here?"

"Have it in the kitchen."

Sal picks up the remote, stops the video, switches off the television, drops the remote bouncing into her chair.

Herbie pauses a moment after she has left. Then, yawning and scratching, he follows her through to the kitchen at the back of the house.

Sal is laying out knives and forks. Herbie sits at the table.

"What they saying on the telly?" he asks her.

"People explaining it. People's reactions to it. Diagrams." She passes his plate to him. The food is already on it.

"This scientist," Herbie presses food onto his fork, "reckoned that the universe would start over again. That it's a perpetual process."

"Do you believe it?" Sal holds her knife and fork unused in her hands. Herbie swallows.

"They say we got to look at the stars tonight."

"They got charts on the telly. Showing you what to look for. Do you believe it?"

"Don't seem we got any choice."

Pulling a ball of tissue from her sleeve Sal lowers her head and begins, quietly, to weep. Herbie makes no move to comfort her. Since her operation this has become the habit of their life. Herbie has since, on occasion, wished that Sal would show more emotion, has as often been glad that she hasn't. He has seen too many hysterical women, and men, to feel pity for them. Always their hysteria has struck him as being untrue, a deliberate lack of self-control. The undemonstrative tears that break through self-control touch him more.

Nor, he knows, does Sal want him to make a fuss. So he stays his side of the table watching her.

"Sorry," she says. "It's just that … well …" an attempt at a smile, "I don't want to die."

"We all got to go some time."

"I know. I know that, but I didn't think we'd all be going together. Me, you, Julie. My mum. All of us going at the same time."

"This scientist I talked to today," Herbie says. "A woman. They've known about it for months. She decided, if the end of the world was coming, what was the point in going on pleasing her husband. And he decided that if he only had that long to live then he was going to go off and have a good time."

"That what you want to do?" Sal asks him. Herbie shakes his head.

"You?"

"No," Sal says. "I can't think what I want to do. The men were in the canteen all day arguing about it. Some are just using it as an excuse to get bolshie. But there was one – he's a little shy man – sits there reading the papers. Then he suddenly gets up, says, 'Sod this!' and he starts to leave. 'Where you going?' they say. 'Bahamas,' he says. 'If all I got is six more days then I'm going to have a bloody good time.' They all laughed."

She picks up her fork, pushes a piece of white chicken around her plate. She lays down her fork. "But everybody took it seriously. If it'd been anybody else I don't think they would've. But he's normally such a serious little man. And all day long I've been trying to think of what I want to do. Really want to do. And I can't think of anything." She squeezes back her tears. "There's nothing I want to do. Not that much. Except be with you. Like we are now."

"I love you." Herbie smiles at her.

"I love you too." She returns the smile, sniffs. "Couple of soppy sods. Look at us." Sal takes up her knife and fork, eats. When their eyes meet they smile at themselves.

Sal pushes her plate away. "There anything you want to do?"

"I been asking myself that on and off all day."

Folding his arms Herbie slides down on the hard kitchen chair, sticks his legs out straight under the table. "And I can't think of anything. 'Cept to go on for longer than six days. Five days now, I suppose." He grunts, "I know I complain about it, but I like my job. I like my home. I like you. Us. I don't want to trade it in for anything else. For something I don't know."

"You want afters?" Sal gets up from the table. "Cold apple pie and cream in the fridge. Or some cake if you want?"

"No thanks."

Sal begins to make coffee. "It's not us I feel sorry for," she says. "I keep thinking of all the worrying we did over Julie. What kind of girl she was going to grow up into. All the trouble we went through with that school. And now she's grown up. Now she's just starting out. And I like her. And not just because she's my daughter. I mean I'd have liked her anyway. I'm proud of her. I'm proud of us. And now just when she's beginning her own life, just when we're beginning to get on our feet, can afford a bit extra here and there, it's all about to stop."

"What she reckon?"

"Can't get hold of her."

Julie is at North London Poly, shares a flat near there.

"You see," Sal puts the coffee cups on the table, sits back down, "we've had our life. We've got we want. Oh, I know not all of it, things could be better, but … it's not too bad. But Julie – she's going to miss out on all that we had. It seems so unfair."

"I was thinking that. And that is the one thing that I do want to do in the next five days – I want to see Julie."

"I still can't believe it's true," Sal says, "that we're sitting here like this talking about it."

"How else?" Herbie gives her a half-smile.

"We're low on flour. I was writing it down on the list. For Saturday. But that's next week's shopping. And we won't be here next week. It doesn't seem possible." She toys with a teaspoon. "You going to stay up and see the stars tonight?"

"Like I keep telling everybody – I don't know what I'm supposed to be looking for. There's always seemed a lot of stars to me."

Herbie sips his coffee.

"Why don't you try Julie now?"

'The whole of human life is illusion. Death alone is real.'
Barry Popieluszko. Psychotic Android Eats: Fire Dragon.

Tuesday: 23:48

Herbie and Sal are lying on their backs in bed. Herbie has one arm behind his head, is staring at the orange rim from the streetlights around the bedroom curtains.

"I'll pack you some sandwiches tomorrow," Sal says. "In case everywhere's closed. You never know. I'll leave them on the table. Don't go off and leave them."

"I won't."

Neither makes the customary moves towards sleep.

"Earlier on," Sal says, "before you came home, they had this cocky young sod on telly. You know the type, sneers at everything. He was going on about religion. 'So where's heaven now if there's no universe?' he said. 'So when's the Second Coming? So when's reincarnation? All of it's cancelled.' he said. 'No reincarnation. No heaven. No hell. All of it's finished.'"

Herbie moves to show that he's heard.

"It annoys me," Sal says. "If it does happen, a lot of people could get comfort from their religion. He's no right to knock it like that. Not now."

Herbie rolls his head to grin at her in the dark. "Didn't know you were religious?"

"I'm not," Sal says. "Well, I am. You know. No need to go to church to be religious. And it's not right his being allowed to say all those things. He was gloating. And if it does end, what's he going to get out of it? That's what I want to know. What's he going to get out of it? It's just plain destructive."

"Probably find a lot of that this week."

Silence again.

"I keep looking around the house," Sal says into the dark. "Keep telling myself that it'll all be gone and that I'm going to miss it. Makes me feel sick inside. Then I tell myself that I won't be here to miss it. And I feel empty."

"I know, love."

A car comes slowly down the street, doesn't stop.

"A van passed me today," Herbie says. "On the Hammersmith flyover. Headlights flashing. Horn blaring. Must've been doing ninety. Know what it had sprayed across the back? 'Who Cares Any More?'"

"Oh Herbie." Sal rolls to him and clutches him.

Herbie takes his arm from behind his head and holds her.

"Saw a kestrel today," he says, when she becomes still. "Hovering over Clapham Common."

'The Egyptians' first calendar was in 2,769BC. What do we know of the future? We who do not even know our past ...'

Barry Popieluszko. The Watcher: Kerala Books.

Wednesday: 08:53

Jim is all alone in the large office. A newspaper is spread open on the desk before him.

"What's on?" Herbie greets him.

Ashtrays and wastepaper bins haven't been emptied. The air in the office is cheesy, unmoving. Mornings, usually the nostrils are sand-blasted by the cleaners' pungent spray: one or two of the detectives have complained of being allergic to it. They have food fads too.

"Nothing." Jim sits back in his chair, studies Herbie.

"Where," Herbie indicates the empty office, "is everyone, then?"

Jim shrugs. "Not turned in."

"Why not?"

"Ah, come on ..." Jim looks about the office, the desk; the same worried search that Mr Trellpott made yesterday. "To tell the truth, I don't know what you and I are doing here. We've got five days left. You tell me, what are the two of us doing here?"

"I want them all on a charge."

"That's everybody but you, me, and the chief. And he's pissed."

"Photographers not in?"

"Not when I phoned."

"The flats?"

"Just me and you. And it's the same throughout the building. Like it's the middle of the bloody night. I don't know what we're doing here."

"Our job."

"Why?"

Herbie doesn't answer, pulls a chair over to Jim's desk, sits facing him. "You know what this is, don't you?" he asks Jim. "I suddenly thought of it last night. It's a story I used to read Julie when she was about three. This is Chicken Licken."

"Chicken what?"

"Chicken Licken. An acorn fell on his head. He thought the sky was falling down, and he went around telling everyone he was on his way to tell the king the sky was falling down. Turkey Lurky I remember. Goosey Lucy. Drakey Lakey. They all went with him to tell the king that the sky was falling down. Know what happened to them?"

Jim doesn't attempt to reply.

"Foxes ate them," Herbie tells him.

Jim is not amused. "This is no kid's story, Herbie."

"We've worked together – what? – three years?" Herbie nods to the newspaper on the desk between them. "You never struck me before as being credulous."

"Nor's any on this team Herbie. We're here because we've got suspicious natures. Because we don't hide from facts. And the fact is that we've all of us only got five days left; and we've none of us seen our families since the weekend before last. For a week and a half now we haven't had time for a quiet drink, even. And suddenly we're told we got five days left. I'm surprised you're here."

"Facts?"

"Fact." Jim holds up one finger. "There's been nothing but this in the papers and on the telly for two whole days now. You think they'd be allowed to get away with it if it wasn't true? There'd be government denials flying about left, right and centre. But not a peep. Not a single solitary peep. You watch any telly last night?"

Herbie shakes his head.

"Every other bod on there," Jim says, "was trying to prove that it wasn't going to happen. None of 'em convinced me. So, fact two," he holds up another finger, "I went out and had a look at the stars for meself."

"How did you know what you were looking for? Except for what they told you?"

"Same tune you were playing yesterday, Herbie. Might have worked then with the others: don't cut any ice with me. Remember I was in the marines, got sent on a survival course or two. Had to find our way by the stars alone. Last night the only configuration I could find was the Plough. All the rest were lost among stars I've never seen before. It's going to happen, Herb."

"I had a look at the sky last night too," Herbie tells him. "When I locked up. Couldn't see a thing. Reflection from the streetlights block out the sky. All you can see is this mauve haze."

"I drove out to Epping Forest. Two in the morning. Roads were packed. But the sky was clear up there. Like it was lit by fairy lights. We got five days left. Believe me. So what are you and I doing here?"

"Our jobs."

Jim sighs. "What job? If accounts don't turn in we won't even get paid this month. And just suppose, by some farfetched miracle, we do collar matey this afternoon, time we get the paperwork done, charge him, it'll all be over. And where do we put him if the uniforms aren't turning in? And what's the point? Supposing we do catch this character who did in Miss Katherine Soames, he's a one-off murderer. He's not likely to kill again before the end of the world. So catching him is deterrence value only. To deter who? When?"

"Always thought you had more stomach for this job."

"Don't give me that old bollocks, Herbie. Like you, I've got commendations for being a dedicated policeman. So've most of the other blokes on this team. And you know as well as I do that it's all total bullshit. They've got young families. Wives, children, girlfriends they want to be with." Jim is unmarried. "With five days left what else do you expect them to do?"

"I didn't expect them to jump so quick. I expected more discipline from them."

"Concentrates the mind wonderfully, knowing exactly when you're going to die. And, face it, what are they? Glorified errand boys. They do their jobs half the time not knowing why they're doing it. You know because you've got overall responsibility. And that's why you're here."

"And you."

"Maybe. But look at it from their point of view. So they don't turn in, so they get put on a charge. It might count against them in promotion. Are any of them likely to get promoted in the next five days? The future's finished. It doesn't count anymore."

"So why are you here? Sergeant?"

"Because I don't have anywhere else to go. And nothing else to do. And that doesn't make me too pleased with my life. What I can't figure out," Jim stares across the desk at Herbie, "is why you're here. You've got a wife, daughter. Why aren't you with them?"

"Sal's gone to work. Julie's got her own life. It's got nothing to do with that." Herbie chops his hand through the air, "I don't want the bastard to get away with it. He brutally murdered that girl. You saw her. So what if in five days we're all going to get wiped out? I want to collar him before then, let him meet the end of the world knowing what a bastard he is." Herbie stands. "Now if you don't want to work any more, you can go. But either way I'm going to catch that bastard. And let me tell you this," Herbie levels a finger at Jim, "if the end of the world doesn't happen then every bloke on this team is going to be on a charge. I'll make bloody sure of it."

Jim stays seated. Then he smiles, folds his newspaper closed. "So how far are we from catching him?"

"Bloody miles."

"What do you want me to do?"

"Look into her college background. Imperial College, South Kensington. Mechanical Engineering. Try to find out who her friends were."

Herbie goes over to the noticeboard. "Talk about her left hand not knowing what her right hand was doing. She spent weekends, holidays with this girl from work. Turns out she hardly knows a thing about her. Never seen her with one bloke. But at one dinner party there was one old college friend. Female. Maybe she told her something about her love life. She had to tell someone. See if she knew matey." Herbie indicates the photograph of the man in the bar. "Anything from the flats?"

"Not so far as I know. What are you up to?"

"I'm off to Newbury. See the parents."

'Will the human race last long enough to learn from its mistakes?'
Barry Popieluszko. Psychotic Android Eats: Fire Dragon.

Wednesday: 11:47

The house is a large bow-fronted semi on the outskirts of Newbury. At the back of the house is a square of lawn bordered with flowers, then a long strip of vegetable garden with, beside it, a double row of short fruit trees. On the shorn lawn is a round metal table. Four wrought metal chairs are tipped up against it.

Mr Soames, in a shapeless khaki shirt and trousers, is bent over his hoe in the vegetable garden.

The house, the garden and the man Herbie recognises from the photographs found in the flat.

Mr Soames raises his head on Herbie's approach. Mr Soames's face is red, the bald head pink. The curly white hair encircling the head looks like a store Santa Claus's cottonwool.

"Mr Soames?" Herbie stops at the edge of the lawn. "Detective Inspector Watkins. Sorry to intrude: I couldn't get an answer from the house."

Mr Soames studies Herbie. He has green eyes. The red face is of broken veins and arteries. "My wife's gone to stay with our son."

"I've come about your daughter. I'm leading the enquiry into her murder."

Mr Soames glances to Herbie's feet on the edge of the lawn. He says nothing.

"I truly am sorry to have to bother you at a time like this," Herbie says, "but we're having some difficulty with our investigation. I was hoping you might be able to help."

Shined hoe handle in hand, Mr Soames now stares expressionlessly directly at Herbie. "Why bother?" he finally asks Herbie.

"Because she was murdered."

"You not heard the news?"

"Yes."

"Then why bother?"

"Why bother with your garden?"

Mr Soames studies Herbie a moment longer, gives an abrupt laugh, explains, "The wife and I decided to spend our last days doing what we wanted. She wanted to be with our grandchildren. This meagre plot is my pride and joy. I want it to be in immaculate condition when it meets the end of the world. What's your reason, Inspector?"

"I told my Sergeant this morning that it was because I didn't want your daughter's murderer to think he'd gotten away with it."

"But he has. In five days' time he'll be treated no different to the rest of us."

"Then on the way here," Herbie continues, "I thought more about it; and it goes deeper than that. My motives as a policeman, I mean. For me it's not retribution. Never has been. Too often I've caught villains only for some clever lawyer to get them acquitted on a technicality. If it'd been justice I'd been after I'd have packed it in years ago. No, for me, I just want to know. To find out how and why and who. Justice has never really entered into it. So long as I knew they were guilty I was satisfied."

"So this is personal?"

"No. It's my job. My wife went to work today. Because that's her job. Habit, maybe. Maybe I just don't want to sit around and twiddle my thumbs until the end of the world. Whatever ... I want to find your daughter's murderer. It's what I've decided to do. Like you're weeding lettuce that are never going to get eaten."

"So how do you suppose I can help you?"

"Your daughter led a very private life, Mr Soames. So private in fact that we can find out nothing about her. And the man who killed her was a friend of hers. A longstanding friend."

"Kate was not the kind of girl who confided in her parents about her lovers."

For a man with a daughter just two days dead, end of the world or not, this man is showing not the least indication of distress – not a blink of the eye, tremble of the vocal chords. Had he disliked her? Family row: already dead to him? Even so ...

"From what I've learnt of your daughter so far, Mr Soames, I don't believe that she was at all promiscuous. There was only one lover. And after murdering her he removed everything from the flat that might incriminate him. Diaries, inscriptions from books, jewellery he'd given her. We have his fingerprints and bloodgroup, but he has no record. And we have not one suspect."

Mr Soames is now a definite suspect. Would have been anyway – in any domestic situation, when a woman becomes the victim of a sexually-oriented murder, all adult male members of her family instantly become candidates for suspicion. Incest/abuse has a long and documented history. And this man (something Herbie had read in the flat yesterday? a letter from her brother?) was a teacher, had therefore chosen to work with children.

Mr Soames has been looking down on his hoe's steel blade. "Do you have any children, Inspector?"

"A daughter."

"Then you know how you worry about such things."

"I know how I worry," Herbie says. "I don't know how you worry."

Mr Soames looks up at Herbie. "How would you feel if she was killed?"

"I don't honestly know," Herbie slowly answers. "Angry?"

"Possibly. Yes. In normal circumstances. But these are, to say the least, exceptional times. No sooner had we learnt that Kate had been killed than we were informed that we were all going to be killed within six days. Any death is difficult for the living to come to terms with. My younger brother died of a stroke two years ago. I still can't accept that he is dead, that I will never see him again. But my brother and I were close. I hardly knew Kate the adult. I don't see how I can help you."

"You knew her better than I did, Mr Soames."

"I would question that. I don't know how much you know about your daughter, but Kate was always secretive. Though that's not strictly true, makes her sound like she enjoyed having secrets. Put it this way – she was always sure what was her business was hers and was no one else's. She certainly didn't confide in me. Nor in her mother."

"Nevertheless you must have known who her friends were at college. You must have known that she had boyfriends."

"How old's your daughter, Inspector?"

"Nineteen."

"Then she's just beginning her own life. Creating a life apart from yours. Basing her judgements not on your values but on her own experiences. Or reacting against you. I've seen children taking up the most peculiar inconsequential beliefs. Peculiar, that is, until I've met their parents. Then all becomes clear. They simply didn't want to own any habit that belonged to their parents, and so they took the contrary view. Are you close to your daughter?"

"Yes."

"Kate was never close to anybody. Even as a child she was hard and unforgiving. She was always impatient with her brother because he was so soft and vacillating. I confess I shared that impatience. But at least he's human."

Mr Soames pauses. "Imagine that strict child growing up, creating her own life … You must now be beginning to feel shut out of your daughter's life. You don't know her friends any more. Who she meets. Maybe she tells you. But it isn't first-hand experience anymore. You don't know. With Kate I never knew."

"She wrote regularly to her brother."

"Did she?"

"Why didn't you tell your son that Kate had been killed?"

"Because my son is sensitive to the point of neurotic. By the time we got over our shock, got around to considering telling him, we were ourselves told that the world was about to end. Why unnecessarily upset him for his last six days on earth?" Mr Soames truculently prods the ground with the hoe. "I hadn't realised they were that close. I told you Inspector, you probably already know more about her than I do."

"I still doubt that, Mr Soames. I may know some things about her that you don't know, but you know many more things that I don't. Did she ever bring any college friends home?"

Mr Soames sticks his hoe deep into the ground, so that it stays upright on its own. "Shall we sit down, Inspector?" He picks his way over rows of green-rose lettuce, red-veined beetroot and fern-like carrot. "Time I had a rest." He taps his chest, "Blood pressure." He reaches the lawn. "Not that it matters now." His voice is lower now that he's closer. "In fact," he winks at Herbie, "on the way back from the station this morning I treated myself to some cigars. Do you?" He proffers the packet to Herbie.

"Thank you, no."

Pulling out two of the garden chairs they sit down. Mr Soames strikes a match and, with a smacking of lips, puffs alight his cigar. He has square-ended fingers, blunt thumbs.

"This question doesn't imply anything, Mr Soames," Herbie says, "but could you tell me where you were on Monday afternoon?"

"Here."

"Can anyone vouch for that?"

"My wife, I suppose."

"Do you know your blood group?"

"Rhesus negative."

"Thank you."

Eyes narrowed by the cigar smoke, Mr Soames looks about him. "Going to rain before night's out. Everything's too sharp. Mind you, the garden needs it. Though, like you say, what's it matter now? Keep wondering whether I should transplant the brussels. Doesn't seem much point. That's the odd thing about gardening. Especially now. Or at my age, anyhow. You're always thinking at least one year ahead. How you're going to rotate your crops, your lawn clippings going into the compost for next year … You garden?"

"Under duress."

"I love it. Hard to explain to someone who doesn't. Though the first beans I picked yesterday were delicious. They might enlighten you. Want some?"

"No thanks."

Mr Soames savours his cigar. Herbie feels the sun burning into his forehead.

"Maybe," Mr Soames says, "ironically now, it's the sense of timelessness gardening gives you. Each season has its jobs, year in year out. Maybe it's just habit. Habits of a lifetime. Habits of life. Like your wife going to work today. At one and the same time it all seems pathetic and yet somehow noble."

"I'm sorry to seem as if I'm interrogating you, but," Herbie fakes a quick smile, "time is short. Did Kate bring any college friends home?"

"She did. One girl. They were very girlish together. Giggling. That sort of thing. Doing each other's hair. That surprised me. I've been trying to think of her name. May have been Barbara. Or

Belinda. But I wouldn't bank on it. I was for forty years a schoolteacher. That meant that for every year I had to learn a hundred-odd new names. If I'd tried to memorise them all permanently I'd have gone mad. As it was after a while they all came to look alike. Which added to the confusion. It may have been Carole." Mr Soames puffs on his cigar. "No. There was alliteration in there somewhere. Carole – Kate. Barbara. No. Sorry."

"Would your wife know?"

"Doubt it. Mrs Malaprop, I'm afraid. Is this girl important?"

"Kate kept in contact with her. A friend of that longstanding she might have confided in."

"Seems impossible, doesn't it?" Mr Soames has his head tilted back looking up at the sky. "In the daylight. Look at those swallows. Come September they won't be flying off again to Africa. Come October," he brings his chin down, points to his fruit trees, "I won't be picking those apples. Come November I won't be raking up those leaves. At night, of course, it's easier to believe. You seen the stars?"

"No."

"With one part of my mind I accept that it really is going to happen. Then I look about me. At that hill over there. At this garden I have made. At those trees. At the flowers in bloom and in bud. And it seems preposterous that they won't all carry on after I am dead. Look at it. It all seems so substantial, so settled. We sleep every night, expect the world to be there when we wake up. The world goes on while we're asleep. We accept our own deaths in that light. I would have come to accept Kate's death in that light. One dies, life goes on. Yet now when I die all will die. Those apricot trees I planted – fifteen years ago – will not now go on fruiting year after year. No one will now pick the fruit not knowing that it was I who planted them. There'll be no fruit to pick. The idea takes some getting used to."

Mr Soames taps the rippled ash off his cigar, grinds the cylinder of ash into the lawn. "Don't get the impression that I didn't enjoy teaching. I did. Like you, I enjoyed my work. When I wasn't just keeping order. When I could see that they were actually learning. When I was passing on some of the accumulated wisdom of mankind. So that they might possibly add to it or, like me, pass it on. Now all that endeavour's come to nought."

Coughing, Mr Soames clears his throat. "Now it all seems such a waste. And it was very comforting, in a sense, to know that life would have gone on without me. That, maybe, in the overall scheme of things, I had served a purpose. And if not that there was a satisfaction even in knowing that I had been a fragment, even without obvious purpose, in the scheme of things. That my existence, unbeknownst to me, had possibly been of some use. In that light, even Kate's death. If you had caught her murderer, had brought him to justice, who can tell what good might ultimately have come of it. But now …"

"Did Kate ever bring any boyfriends home?"

"One. Years ago, though."

"He still might know something."

"A writer. No Shakespeare, mind you. To be honest I didn't like him. Told Kate that he wouldn't become Dylan Thomas just by drinking as much as he had. There again," with a wave of his cigar Mr Soames dismisses what he has just said, "if he was playing a role then so too was I. Until now I've never seen myself as being very sociable. I've always kept my distance. In fact I've rather prided myself on being anti-social. The staff-room grouch. The potting shed hermit. But this week I see I've been as gregarious as the next man. As herdlike as the great unwashed in a bank holiday traffic jam. These last two days I've seen that I have subjugated my entire life to the welfare of my species. And I thought I was just doing my job. While all my life I have been unwittingly, like you, a servant of the people."

"Can you remember this writer's name?"

"Barry   Something.   Polish   name.   Could've   been Czechoslovakian. Though he was English born and raised. He gave my wife one of his books. Because he wrote her name in it she kept it. It's indoors. Not Conrad by a long chalk. And she talked about art."

"Your wife?"

"Kate. Called him an artist. A talentless hack overfond of the bottle, if you ask me. I was glad when she ditched him."

"This him?" Herbie shows him the photograph.

"Appropriately enough, in a pub."

"Is it him?"

"It is."

"Any subsequent boyfriends?"

"I guessed there must be some. Or one. She never mentioned any."

"I think she may have been having a long term affair with a married man."

"Now that does surprise me. Kate wasn't one to share. Had very clear ideas on right and wrong. Would explain why she kept him quiet, though."

"When did you last see her?"

"Three months ago. Early spring. Crocuses were out. I was ill. She came home four weekends in a row. Reorganised the house, patronised her mother, nursed me. The pity of grown children being kind to their aged parents. Being patient with them. I don't make a very good invalid."

"Have you been to her flat?"

"In Victoria? Afraid not. The wife stayed there once. A Christmas shopping spree. Kate was busy. My wife said – what's the expression? – that she wasn't made to feel welcome."

Herbie can't imagine himself being that distant from Julie. Nor she being that closed off from him. Did Kate Soames and this puffing old git never laugh together?

"Do you like opera?"

"That's how they surprise you. I've no musical inclination whatsoever. Kate came to that all by herself. Could never understand her predilection for art and artists. She had such a good scientific brain on her. Yet she got taken in by all that woolly-minded art nonsense."

"What did you teach?"

"History. Which ends in four days' time. No future, no more history."

Mr Soames screws his cigar stub among the crumbs of soil on the yellow sole of his shoe. "The only lesson left for man to learn from history is that he needn't have bothered learning it."

'The novelist has to divine, and to define each individual's relationship with the universe, their measurement of time.'

Barry Popieluszko. Raw As Birth: White Swan.

Wednesday: 15:04

The traffic lights sink from red to amber into green. Herbie goes with the queue of cars, crosses the wide Cromwell Road, enters the approach to Earls Court Road.

The cars caterpillar to a halt. Herbie waits. The cars before him move forward a few meters. He closes up behind them, and waits.

From somewhere ahead comes a mushy boom, not sharp enough for an explosion. Herbie tries to look around the car in front.

Black smoke is beginning to pile up between the canyon walls of Earls Court Road. Herbie glances at the drivers in the cars around him. All are stretching up trying to see through the cars ahead of them. A taxi driver to the rear of him can see, is giving a running commentary to his two passengers. A sports car two cars ahead of Herbie pulls out of the lane and, two wheels on the pavement, makes for a turning on the left. The road leading off has 'no entry' signs on either corner. A lamp-post stops the sports car. The cars before Herbie make no move to fill the vacated space.

Black smoke is now towering out of the dun-coloured canyon into the sharp blue sky.

Herbie undoes his seat-belt, leans across to the passenger seat to see around the drivers of the cars in front. Further down, where the road narrows before the tube station, a car is lying on its side and spouting orange flames. Broken glass lies about it. A shouting crowd flank it. Behind their dark flickering legs lies a twisted body.

One of a crowd of drunks, Herbie guesses, has been knocked over by the now burning car. The crowd must have dragged the driver out, have turned the offending car onto its side and set fire to it. A pub next to the accident has had its windows smashed.

Blaring its horn at the crowd, a small delivery van at the head of the traffic queue tries to squeeze past the burning car. The crowd in the shadow of the smoke does not part. Their faces turn towards the white van. From out of this crowd two youths jump onto the van's narrow bonnet and begin to kick its windscreen. Glass chips spray out on either side of the van. The driver tries to scramble from his door. He is thrown through the crowd onto the pavement.

The crowd now pauses, seems uncertain what to do next. The driver is not attacked. Instead, as soon as the two youths have leapt from the front of the van, the crowd begins to rock it.

The white van too is turned onto its side.

The crowd is whooping and shouting now, the senseless manic yells of a football mob. When they see the driver of the car, which is now at the head of the queue, fall scrambling from his car door, they, laughing, advance on that car.

Some others of the crowd have gathered about the car, and the one beside it, are tapping on the windows telling the drivers to get out. Both cars are tipped onto their sides.

All around Herbie drivers panic.

Two cars in the other lane shoot off down a narrow turning to the right. The car immediately beyond that turning reverses back, meets the next oncoming car. They smash together in the entrance to the turning. More cars are frantically trying to reverse from the advancing mob.

The sports car that had gone onto the pavement now begins to shunt its way between two cars and the lamp-post, but succeeds only in jamming itself and another car between the two 'no entry' signs. As with the turning on the right the other cars pressing on the crashed cars leave them no room for manoeuvre. Unable to extricate themselves the air becomes blue with exhaust fumes and the stink of burning rubber.

In the open space provided by the two drivers who got away, the taxi tries to turn and get back to the Cromwell Road. But even its tight lock doesn't have enough room to complete its circle; and the cars retreating from the mob fill the space it used to partially turn.

The driver in front of Herbie is signalling him to go back. Herbie looks behind.

The traffic has piled up the width of the Cromwell Road and back up towards Kensington. Both carriageways of the Cromwell Road, so far as he can see and hear from the caterwauling of horns, are getting a tailback.

The girl in the small green car directly behind him is studying her rearview and wing mirrors.

Herbie shrugs at the flushed driver of the car in front of him, looks around him to the advancing mob.

Two more cars have been tipped onto their sides. None, except the first, has been set on fire. One of the drivers is trying to fight the mob. He is being pushed indifferently aside, a woman laughing at him. Two tall men are attempting, good-naturedly, to placate him.

The crowd is more intent on attacking the traffic. And, wiping their hands on their clothes, they proceed to the next two cars.

Some at the rear of the mob are ransacking an off-licence. Cans of beer, bottles of wine and spirits are being passed up to those at the forefront of the mob. Heads are being tilted back.

They are not all young people. Among them are men Herbie's age, shirtsleeves rolled up; a grey-haired, plump woman with a white handbag on her arm. One big party.

A thin man with a shoulderbag comes walking alongside the traffic jam. On seeing the extent of the mob he slows a moment. But on he goes, his back straight, his step springing off his toes.

Herbie knows well what that man is feeling, that almost physical energy a mob gives off, like a radiation of pure adrenalin, be they football supporters, peace demonstrators, or a spontaneous mob of drunks like these.

Reaching them, the man, with a perky little smile, passes them by, skips and dances between those he cannot avoid. His smile one of placation, of self-nullity.

Thirst slaked, the crowd place their cans and bottles on the ground, politely ask the driver of the next car to leave. He remonstrates, pleads with them. He is, smiling, pushed aside. A girl gives him a bottle. The bottle hanging in his hand he watches as, practised now, they bend their backs to his car.

"One. Two. Three. Heave!" Herbie hears them, and their triumphant shout as the car crunches onto its side.

He glances to his mirror.

The girl has got out of her green car and is shouting at the drivers of the cars behind her, waving them to go to her left.

Herbie studies her: a neat tidy woman. Age somewhere between twenty-five and thirty. A cool contained lady. Except for the blonde hair, another Katherine Helen Soames. Does she keep a diary? Why didn't Kate drive? Should have been an early accomplishment for such a polished young lady like Katherine Helen Soames.

"One. Two. Three. Heave!"

This car, an antique Riley, doesn't make it onto its side, falls back down onto its wheels.

The crowd, shouting, scatters. The exhaust snaps dustily under it. The owner looks on, hands clasped as if in prayer. More of the crowd come to help lift it.

The driver of the car in front of Herbie is frantically waving at him. Herbie looks to his mirror. The girl in the green car has reversed back to the Cromwell Road.

Herbie fills the space. A cheer goes up from the mob. The Riley is on its side. The cars reverse again.

The traffic from Kensington is now turning right to go west along Cromwell Road. While they are doing that the cars that have been jammed in the Earls Court Road are reversing into Cromwell Road, then they too are driving west.

Herbie reverses again, stops. The driver of the car in front of Herbie makes a motion of wiping sweat from his brow. Herbie gives him a sympathetic smile.

The mob has now shifted the tipped cars around to form a barricade. Some youths stand waving shirts and shouting atop the upturned cars.

When the lights behind the queue of cars change, they reverse again. Herbie lets the girl turn. He thoughtfully follows her west down the Cromwell Road. He saw not one uniform in Earls Court.

'You (human) are as existentialist as the seasons.'
Barry Popieluszko. Happy Robot Goes Cosmic: Fire Dragon.

Wednesday: 17:41

Herbie dials the Southampton number that Directory Enquiries gave him. Sal is singing to herself in the kitchen. The ringing tone monotonously repeats itself. Herbie rearranges his notebook on the low table before him.

"Yes?" A man's voice, brusque.

"Could I speak to Mrs Soames, please?"

"Who's calling?"

"Detective Inspector Watkins, New Scotland Yard."

"This about Kate?"

"It is."

"I don't see what my wife can tell you that I haven't already told you."

"Sorry, Mr Soames, it was your mother I wanted to talk to. I went to Newbury today and I saw your father, but your mother had already left. And with the state of the traffic I didn't really want to drive to Southampton today."

"All right. But I don't see the point."

"Tell her it will only take a minute." But Mr Ben Soames has already gone.

Herbie listens to children shouting in another room. Adult voices. Anxious female question and abrupt male answer. Another woman's voice is raised in angry complaint. A cursing shout from the man.

The phone clatters as it is taken up.

"Hello?" Herbie says. "Hello? Mrs Soames?"

"Yes?" a worried old woman.

"Detective Inspector Watkins here. I'm sorry to bother you but I'm leading the investigation into Kate's death, and I was wondering if you could help me with some background information."

"I don't see how."

"It won't take a minute."

"We were just about to sit down to tea."

Nervous, Mrs Soames sounds unsure of her own speech and her own mind. Bullied by her husband, Herbie guesses, bossed about by her son. Should he join with them in browbeating her? He decides not: she can too easily drop the phone on him.

"Did Kate talk to you about her current boyfriend?"

"Current boyfriend?"

"The man she was living with? Going out with?"

"Was she?"

"Yes, Mrs Soames. You've no idea?"

"No."

"Do you know a Barry Popieluszko?"

"Barry? Yes, but … Oh, I haven't seen him for … Oh, years now. What's he got to do with it?"

"Did Kate mention him recently?"

"Not that I can think of. Why can't you let her rest in peace? I mean, what's the good of it now?"

"It's not her I want to disturb, Mrs Soames. It's her murderer I don't want to let rest in peace."

"I know, but what good will it do? What's done's done."

Background voices, sharp and meant to be heard.

"Where were you Monday afternoon, Mrs Soames?"

"Monday afternoon? I went into Reading."

"Reading? What time did you get home?"

"Can't say for sure. I know I was late. Got caught up in the rush hour."

"Did your husband go with you?"

"He doesn't like shopping."

"Where did he go?"

"Go? Nowhere."

"He was at home?"

"Of course."

"What's your blood group, Mrs Soames?"

"My blood group? I've no idea. Why?"

"Do you know your husband's?"

"Yes. It's an odd one. Would be. They always want him to give blood. Didn't he show you his badges?"

"No. Did he often go to stay with Kate?"

"Stay with Kate? No, he never goes anywhere."

A woman impatiently calls her. The man again shouts. A child screams its tears.

"I've got to go now."

"Mrs Soames?"

"Yes?"

"Why didn't Kate learn to drive?"

"What's that got to do with it?"

"Every aspect of this ..."

"Look I've got to go now."

"One last question please. Kate's college friend. Came to stay with you. What was her name?"

"Oh ... it was ... Barbara? Yes, Barbara."

"Surname?"

"Oh ... I've no idea."

"Do you know where she lives?"

"London, somewhere. It was years ago."

"You're sure it was Barbara?"

The woman's insisting voice calls her again.

"Yes. I've got to go. 'Bye."

'A human life is always in a state of becoming – becoming adult, becoming parent, becoming older. Dead it arrives at.'

Barry Popieluszko. Raw As Birth: White Swan.

Wednesday: 20:39

Herbie reaches over to Sal's armchair for the remote control, switches off the video and telly.

The front door has closed on voices. Sal comes into the living room arching an eyebrow at whoever is behind her. Julie, bright-eyed and smiling, comes past her – instantly familiar – to kiss Herbie on the cheek. Her hair is long and dark. Strands catch in Herbie's bristled chin as she draws away.

"Dad, this is Peter."

A boy stands in the living room doorway; unzipped leather jacket, brown sweatshirt, jeans, black fur-lined leather boots. Tall and thin, he has blond hair, straight black eyebrows, brown eyes and red lips.

Julie signals him.

"Pleased to meet you." He advances on Herbie with his hand self-consciously outstretched.

Herbie cumbersomely extricates himself from the armchair, shakes the hand. All bone, no flesh.

"You at college with Julie?" Herbie asks him.

Peter, blushing, is now shaking hands with Sal. "Yes."

"I'll make coffee," Sal says, and leaves.

Herbie is smiling down on them both. His social smile. "Sit down," he says, resumes his seat. In the kitchen water gushes. Peter and Julie sit side by side on the sofa.

"Your Mum," Herbie looks to Julie, "said you'd phoned. Said you sounded mysterious."

"I just told her to wait and see." Julie, flushing, glances to Peter.

"What you studying?" Herbie asks Peter.

"I was doing electronics."

"Was?"

"Place has practically closed down."

"Of course." Herbie nods.

In the kitchen a tray is being prepared.

"Julie said you were a policeman," Peter says

"Detective," Julie corrects him.

"I'd have thought," Herbie winks at her, "she'd have kept that to herself in college."

"Exact opposite."

Peter does not have a London accent.

"Where you from?"

"All over."

"His father's in the Air Force."

"But I went to school here. In Dorset. Holidays I stayed with my father. In Germany. Cyprus. Hong Kong. Belize."

"Seen a bit of the world, then?"

"Peter can speak Chinese," Julie proudly informs her father.

"Only enough to get by," Peter tells her.

"Not only," Julie says, "can he ask for chopsticks in Chinese, he can use them as well."

Sal brings in the coffee tray. Herbie positions the low table for her. Sal pours for everyone, asks Peter if he takes sugar.

"One, please."

"So what brings you around tonight?" Sal asks Julie.

"Well …" Julie draws herself, knees together, up to the edge of the sofa. "Sounds ridiculous now." She laughs, her showy laugh, "It's the end of the world."

Sal glances anxiously, guiltily to Herbie. Life is fragile: Sal knows that. She had very nearly lost them all once. That, though, had been her losing. And they'd have lost her; but they themselves, with other lives, would have carried on. This, though …

"What about it?" Herbie asks Julie.

Peter concentrates on balancing his coffee cup.

"We were talking," Julie shrugs her narrow shoulders, "me and Peter, about how best to spend our last few days. What we'd most like to do. Climb Everest." She giggles. "Pilot a plane. We agreed it had to be something we'd never done before. Today we decided. We'd see Naples and die."

Peter and Julie glance quickly to one another. A lovers' glance full of secrets, seeking reassurance.

Julie's boyfriends up to now Herbie has consciously patronised. That had seemed the purpose of Julie bringing them home – to test them against her father. Consequently Herbie and Sal had allowed themselves to be amused by them, which it appeared was what Julie had intended. This one though, Herbie senses, is different, has an importance all to himself.

Herbie had anticipated being resentful, jealous of his only daughter's chosen man. Instead, sizing Peter up now, he finds himself wanting to befriend this stranger, finds himself pleased for Julie; and yet once again proud of her – in that she has found someone other than her parents to love her.

He smiles at them. "That's it?"

"That's it." Julie, smiling as of old at him, puts her head to one side, the familiar fond gesture now touching Peter's shoulder. Peter smiles apologetically at Herbie.

"Don't be so bloody ridiculous," Sal says.

Herbie watches Julie change in a moment from being soft and happy to stiff and defensive.

"We're not being ridiculous, Mum. We're leaving tonight."

"And how're you going to get there? On that motorbike?"

"Probably the only way we will get there. Only way we got here tonight. Honestly, there's riots going on everywhere," she tells Herbie. "Wasn't one shopfront in Lambeth that wasn't smashed. Even those with grills. And cars all over the place. Drunks and crowds everywhere. Like New Year's Eve in Trafalgar Square. On the motorbike, though, we just went around it all."

"And how long have you known him?"

"Just over a week," Peter answers.

"I've known you longer than that," Julie tells him. "He means we've been together just over a week. But I've met him around college before."

"And after just one week you're going to go swanning off to Naples with him?"

"His name is Peter, Mum."

"What do your parents make of it?" Sal asks Peter.

"I can't get through to my father. He's on Ascension," he tells Herbie. "They said they were on operations. My mother," he addresses himself to Sal, "left us when I was six. I've no idea where she is."

"You got continental insurance for your bike?" Herbie asks him.

"I went to Germany at Easter. I was going again this summer. See friends there. My father would have been there, but last week he was transferred."

"He's in the Air Force," Herbie tells Sal.

"Anyway, it worked out cheaper to insure for the whole year than it did for two, maybe three, separate periods."

"I've only got one serious question." Herbie looks to the pair of them, "What if the world doesn't end in four days? If it's all been a big con?"

"Then we'll have seen Naples and had a week's holiday," Julie replies.

Julie went to Majorca for a fortnight last summer with a friend, had saved the money working in Sal's canteen. Sal had enjoyed working with Julie.

"I suppose you'll be sharing bedrooms," Sal says.

"If we can find one," Julie defiantly chirps.

"Where else will you sleep?" Herbie asks.

"We've got sleeping bags."

"Groundsheet?"

"We got a sheet of plastic," Peter answers the practical question.

"One sheet," Sal accuses.

"Sal ..." Herbie says. "We've all of us got four days left. Why argue?"

"When you thinking of leaving?" Sal asks Julie.

"Now." Julie pales. "We just called by to tell you."

"Spend the night here," Sal says. "I can soon make up a bed for Peter ..."

"We got a ferry to catch, Mum."

Sal, having started to rise, sits back heavily, covers her face and weeps. Julie crosses to her. Kneeling, she peels Sal's hands from her face,

"Don't cry, Mum. Not you."

Tears are filling Julie's large brown eyes. Herbie and Peter look away from the weeping women. Herbie clears his throat.

"How you fixed for money?" he asks Peter.

"We both cashed the last of our allowances."

"I'll see what I've got." Herbie stands. "Money's always handy."

In the kitchen Herbie takes his wallet from his jacket pocket. He can hear Sal apologising in the living room. After a moment's hesitation Herbie empties the wallet.

On the hall floor, lying together like two cock-eyed Easter eggs, are a black helmet and a blue helmet.

"Here you are." He gives the money to Julie. "Should be able to change it on the ferry."

Through her tears Julie looks at the wad of notes in her hand.

"Where'd you get all this?"

"For touts. Carry-outs for the team. Always have enough on me. Now you take care. Both of you. And phone us if you can."

"We'd better be going." Peter stands uncomfortably by.

"Good luck." Herbie clasps him by the hand.

"I'll take care of her, Mr Watkins." Peter staunchly declares. For reply Herbie ruffles his dry thick hair.

In the hallway Julie and Peter zip up their creaking jackets, pull on their gloves, don their helmets. Julie's is the blue helmet. The jacket, she tells them, is sort of borrowed.

Julie hugs first her mother, then her father. The helmet is cold against Herbie's cheek.

The four of them troop out to the small red motorbike, its nylon panniers bulging. The clear sky is darkening into evening, windows and doors of the houses outlined clearly against the stark lines of the pointed brickwork.

Peter mounts and starts the bike. Julie straddles the pillion and clasps him around the waist.

"Mind how you go." Herbie winks at Peter, imitates a policeman's kneebend. Peter grins at him.

"Take care." Sal touches Julie's arm. Julie nods, attempts a smile.

Sal and Herbie watch the bike go up the street between the parked cars. Its red brake light comes brightly on as it reaches the junction, goes off as it stops.

"Romantic fools," Herbie says.

Cars pass on the main road.

"We don't know a thing about him," Sal worries.

"She's not a part of our life any more." Herbie puts his arm around Sal's shoulders. "She's making her own life now."

"All four days of it."

The distant dark figure on the back of the motorbike lifts her thin arm. Herbie raises his hand. Sal sobs and waves furiously. The motorbike turns right.

'The future neither justifies nor condemns the past, it merely follows it.'
Stephen Vizinczey. In Praise Of Older Women.

'Is the world perfect today? It is not. The past is therefore nothing to be proud of ... '
Barry Popieluszko. Happy Robot Goes Cosmic: Fire Dragon.

Thursday: 10:28

In his small office Mike is leaning by the window looking out at the rain. His hair is cut short, a bald patch thinning out from the crown, white collar tight on his wide neck.

"This morning," he says, "I can well believe it's the end of the world. All I can see from here is wet smoke. What's under that smoke I don't know. Cars seem favourite. House or two maybe. One thing's for certain – you won't see any fire engines."

"Thought the rain had freshened the air a bit." Herbie sits down. "Your note said you wanted to see me."

"Not you in particular." Mike does not turn away from the window. "Anyone would've done. Just that I was beginning to get the feeling that I was the last man alive in this soddin' building."

"Yeah. Sorry I'm late. Ran out of cash, had to go to the bank. Lucky I was there early. Queues a mile long. And they're checking everyone's account by hand before they let 'em draw money. And, of course, they're shortstaffed. And everyone's only making withdrawals. Looked like it was the same with the building societies. Cashpoints were all empty, somebody told me."

Mike, uninterested, has continued to stare out the window.

"Thought you might want to know," Herbie says, "what I was up to."

"And what are you up to?" Mike asks.

"Still the Katherine Soames case. Not proving as easy as I first thought. Boyfriend was one dark horse. I'm off to see an old boyfriend today. Camden. See if he knows who his successor might've been."

"What about that North London job?"

"Nobody there. And even Jim hasn't turned in this morning. I'll have a nose round after I've seen matey."

"You don't think the world's going to end, then, Herbie?"

Mike is watching Herbie in the window reflection. Herbie pushes the chair away from the desk, stretches his legs out before him.

"What's it matter either way? Whether it ends or not? If it doesn't end, I'm here doing my job. And if it does end, I'm here doing my job. Either way I'm here now."

"Want to know why I'm here, Herbie?" Mike turns to face him.

A cynic beyond his years, Mike has a clever, sad face. Herbie occasionally finds himself feeling sorry for him, as often exasperated.

"Why are you here?" Herbie flatly asks of him.

"I'm here, like I was here yesterday, and I was here the day before, waiting for that phone to ring." Mike points dramatically to the two telephones on his desk. "Waiting for someone to tell me it's all been one great big fucking mistake! That," he bangs the flat of his hand on the desk, leans over Herbie, "is why I'm here."

Although Mike has neither slurred his speech, nor staggered, his drunkenness is apparent in the exaggerated way he resumes his leaning by the window. This man sober is calm and poised and contained, a PR man's dream of a police officer.

"It's been all right for you, Herbie. You got this abstract notion of what a policeman should be. Me? All that's ever bothered me's been promotion."

"Bothered me enough in the past."

"Not like it has me. *All* that's bothered me's been promotion."

Mike is younger than Herbie.

"Ethics, principles, personal loyalties, all have gone by the board. Number of times I've kept my mouth shut when I should've opened it. But no, I've been a good boy, and good boys don't speak out against their superiors. Good boys don't tell their superiors disagreeable things. Yessir! Nossir! Three Bags Full Sir! I've taken the credit off men like you. And got promoted and disliked for it. You tell me of anyone who trusts me."

"I trust you," Herbie says.

Mike grunts, "You mean you know where you stand with me. But you tell me now what friggin' good all my schemin's done me. Go on, tell me." He turns from the window to again face Herbie. "It's no secret, is it, Herbie, that I've always got my eye on promotion? And not because I think I can do things better. Oh no, because I want to be the Big I Am. Now I ask myself what the fuck for? All that yessiring, if you say so Sir, that's very funny Sir. What for? For fuck all."

"We've all of us done that."

Embarrassed for him, Herbie studies his own feet. "There's not a man on the force who hasn't decided, at some time or other, silence is golden. I've done it. Would've done me no good, nor anyone else, to have said anything."

"It's more than that with me, Herbie. I've dropped mates in it – deliberately. So that I would appear a good officer. The bullshit I've stood through – takes a special kind of courage to rat on your own colleagues. And I've since handed it out. Almost word for bloody word to another up-and-coming creep. But you, Herbie, you got promotion because you're a good policeman. I've licked arses to get here. I haven't seen you lick one."

"If you weren't my superior officer I wouldn't be sitting here now. You're just down." Herbie draws his feet under him, sits forward. "We're all of us hard on ourselves when we're down."

"Bollocks, Herbie. I mortgaged my pride to the future. Now I've got none. I sacrificed my marriage to my career. Now I've got none. I put in all the hours I could, was there whenever I was needed. Now I've got no career, got no marriage."

"That's not only you." Herbie pulls a face. "Policemen's marriages are notoriously short. Policewomen's even shorter. Goes with the job."

"She was a policewoman." Mike laughs. Stops. "Your marriage is still going."

"I've been lucky." Herbie stands.

"Seen the state of the roads?" Mike waves an arm at the window. "I had to make six detours this morning. Had to bulldoze my way past three wrecks – just to get here. What the hell's it coming to Herbie when a policeman can't get to work?"

"Most of the main roads are still open. Trouble is there's no uniforms anywhere. Or not enough anyway."

"Sport too," Mike says.

"Sport?" Herbie shifts impatiently.

"I've been West London badminton champion twice now, you know. Go for a run every morning I can. I like watching sports. Now all those records that've been broken mean nothing. Absolutely nothing."

"Look, Mike, I've got to get on. If I can crack this one before the weekend, I'll go out a happy man."

"And just what're you going to do with him if you do catch him?"

"Even if I have to lock him up myself, he'll meet the end of the world where he belongs."

"See," Mike says to the window and the weather, "you're a policeman. Me? I've been toying with the idea of telling the Commissioner to go fuck himself. If I can find him."

'The present, with its compromises and grit, is always sleazy. Memory's past owns clean lines. The future is similarly uncluttered. This present, though, has sticky fingers and greasy skin ... Yes, as usual, this here & now most definitely lacks glamour.'

Barry Popieluszko. Raw As Birth: White Swan.

Thursday: 11:50

Herbie stands bareheaded in the rain outside a flat-fronted terrace house of faded orange brick.

The yellow door has no porch. In the narrow space between the square front window and a low wall are two full dustbins, their crooked black rubber lids sitting awry on top of the bulging plastic bags.

Herbie again presses the bell button. The yellow door opens.

"What d'you want?"

The man from the photograph is standing before him.

The dark brown hair is not now so long, nor as thick. Flat on the crown. Thin face, unshaven, wide mouth, grey eyes, straight eyebrows, high cheekbones. Mid-forties, slim build, average height. Faded jeans, grey sweatshirt.

He has one hand on the edge of the door. Long hand, long thin fingers.

"Barry Popieluszko?"

"What d'you want?"

Herbie digs under his mac for his ID. "Detective Inspector Watkins. Can I come in?"

The man doesn't move. "What for?"

"I'm conducting the investigation into the unlawful killing of Katherine Helen Soames. I was hoping that you might be able to help me with my enquiries."

Barry Popieluszko stares at Herbie. The cold rain dribbles down the back of Herbie's collar, makes Herbie's shoulderblades squirm. Barry Popieluszko steps back from the door. "Better come in."

In the hall Herbie has to step around bicycles. A pile of coats is hung over the bottom stair post. Barry Popieluszko leads the way through to a back room.

In the room is a plain wood table, an odd assortment of hard chairs. A tricycle, brick trolley, and other bits of children's toys lie around the floor. A large television sits askew upon a sideboard. On top of the television, and on every other flat surface, even the chairs, are newspapers, books, magazines, opened envelopes.

On the rear of the house is a kitchen extension. The sink is stacked high with crockery. Smells of old cooking.

Barry Popieluszko turns to face Herbie, the plain wood table between them. "How am I able to help you?"

Herbie shakes the rain out of his collar. "Do you dislike the police?"

Barry Popieluszko thinks about his reply. "Not particularly. In fact you've got my every sympathy. I simply don't like bad policemen."

"Nor do I."

"And I don't like people who deny they exist instead of stamping on them."

"Nor do I. So why the hostility?"

Barry Popieluszko makes a quick nervous gesture, half apologetic. "You interrupted me."

"Of course," Herbie smiles, "you were writing. I'll try to take up as little of your time as possible. We've none of us that much left."

"I was just thinking of stopping for lunch anyway." Another nervous gesture. "Want some?"

Herbie tries not to look towards the stack of unwashed dishes. "Wouldn't say no to a cup of coffee."

"Right."

Barry Popieluszko goes into the kitchen, begins picking cups out of the sink.

"And if you've got a towel I could dry my hair with?"

"Bathroom. Up the stairs. First door you come to."

The carpet on the stairs is threadbare. The bath has two dirt rings. The basin is likewise smeared. Herbie sniffs at the green towel hanging behind the door. It is fabric-conditioner clean. He rubs at his hair, fingercombs it in the mirror. On a shelf at the end of the bath is an almost empty packet of disposable nappies.

On the landing is a heap of children's and baby's clothes. In one bedroom is a cot and a single bed, both unmade, with soft toys, torn paper and books over the floor.

In the other room, a double bed, unmade. Some women's clothes on a chair. Some on the floor.

Downstairs Herbie glances through the open door into the front room. Shelf upon shelf of books. A desk behind the door. The desk light is still switched on, pen lying across a sheet of half-written paper. Stink of cigarette smoke. Full ashtray. Short stubs. Books and papers have been laid out on the floor.

The plain wood table has been cleared of newspapers. A steaming mug of coffee stands on it. Barry Popieluszko is in the kitchen grilling toast.

"Have a good nose round?" he smiles at Herbie.

"Thanks," Herbie says.

Through the window is a neat flower garden enclosed by brick walls, the rain dripping from the pots and plants hung on the walls.

"You do the garden?" Herbie asks.

"My wife does."

"Where is she?"

"Took the kids to Scarborough. Going to spend their last few days at the seaside building sandcastles with their grannies. Not my idea of fun."

"You from up North?"

"Originally. My grandfather was a Pole, if you're wondering how I got my monicker."

"Pronunciation worried me a bit."

"My teachers used to call me Poppy. Pricks. Barry'll do if it bothers you."

He brings two rounds of toasted sandwiches to the table, studies Herbie as he sits down. "Can I ask you some questions?"

"Go ahead." Herbie opens his palms. "Seems only fair."

Barry Popieluszko composes himself. "How was Kate murdered?"

"Battered to death with a metal statuette."

"Where?"

"In her flat."

"When?"

"Monday afternoon. Where were you Monday afternoon?"

"Here. So was my wife. How did you find me?"

"Standard police procedure."

"Computer?" A disapproving frown.

"No." Herbie grins. "Telephone directory."

"What I was getting at," Barry Popieluszko feigns annoyance, "was how did you come to be looking for me?"

"A photograph of you in her flat. Then Kate's father told us that you'd been to stay with them once. You gave Kate's mother one of your books."

"But why look for me? Do you think I did it?"

"Not now. The murderer had large flat thumbs."

Barry Popieluszko examines his thumbs. One is nicotine stained.

"When did you last see Kate?" Herbie asks him.

"About four years ago. When we split up. I got another question first – why are you bothering?"

"Was waiting for that." Herbie smiles. "And I was hoping to get mine in first. Why are you bothering writing? Because, unless it's in a newspaper tomorrow, nobody's ever going to read it."

"True."

Barry Popieluszko bites into his sandwich, thinks, speaks through it. "Not getting read has never stopped anyone writing. People can write for tens of years without hope of getting published. I did. It's like a drug. Once started it's hard to stop. Come to depend on it. Now if I don't write of what happens to me it doesn't become real. My thoughts become clear only on paper. Unless viewed through a frame of words nothing's real for me anymore. Ask any unpublished writer ever. I suppose most must have hoped to have been read some time by somebody who would be in sympathy. But there's plenty more like me who've just got to get it out of them. Each little thought, put it on paper and forget it. Keep our dreams inside us, they fester and poison. On unread paper they can damage no one. Worse still, if we didn't write, we might live our imaginations. Least, this way, we do it quietly. That's my excuse," he cuts himself short. "What's yours?"

Herbie has been watching him while he talked – hands flicking in unfinished gestures, eyebrows raised, face pointing after words, the eyes self-absorbed, talking half to himself, half to Herbie.

The confiding gush of a lonely man. Or the outpourings of shock.

The man's adrenalin is up, pupils dilated, face pale. Some talk their way out of shock, others go dumb. No point pushing him, Herbie tells himself. Relax. Let it come.

Barry Popieluszko chews as rapidly as Herbie talks.

"Got no excuse," Herbie tells him. "It's my job. And I like my work. Anything wrong with that?"

"Commendable." Barry Popieluszko swallows. "Lucky, too. There's a lot of aimless people suddenly about. The Great God Future is dead. The Great God Future who promised everything if only we sacrificed today. He's dead. No more carrots, no more sticks. Must have come as quite a shock to the majority of people how much the future dominated their lives."

"Doesn't seem to have bothered you much."

"Like the sennapod said to the suppository, when you gotta go you gotta go." (Wasn't much of a joke: Herbie doesn't smile). "I'm a writer. As such I've probably made as much of a study of people as you. You must know that the present doesn't exist for most people. When I was ... When I am ... We're none of us here. All of us living back in, forward in, some other time. Cheated of our every real moment by our own imaginations. Most people, I'm sure, haven't realised before now how little we live in the present: we are what we believe we will become. And suddenly there's no more becoming. The future's been whipped out from under their feet. Crime, as you know, is concerned solely with the future. Bribes, threats, blackmail: all employ the future, the unknown future, as an accomplice."

"What about nostalgia?" Herbie asks brightly. "If, like you say, the future owned everyone, there'd be no such thing as nostalgia."

"True. Yes, true. And there are those who view even yesterday with nostalgia. But there are more who look forward, who view even the day ahead with expectancy. Backward-lookers reminisce idle, while forward-lookers do, try to turn every moment to advantage, make something of it. A step along the way. Got no definite idea where they're going, 'cept they aren't there yet. While yer nostalgics can't remember exactly when life was so good, still they have this feeling that life was better some time before, after all, things happened then, didn't they? And don't forget this – even nostalgics have a stake in the future – they want to recreate those halcyon days. Seen the papers today?"

"Haven't had a chance."

"All wars have stopped. Right around the globe. A few odd shots being fired here and there; old scores being settled, a few slates being wiped clean. But that's all. This world at the moment is in a state of unofficial ceasefire. Three days from the end of the world, Inspector, and peace has been declared. And no wars, no news. The media's preoccupation with calamity has paled into total insignificance faced with our imminent extinction."

"You're enjoying this?"

"No, not a bit. But I do feel as if I've been proved right. Know why society's disintegrating? Because it was only held together by appearances. By all of us doing our best to appear normal. At least, not to appear abnormal. Now who cares what anyone else thinks? We had no deeper philosophy binding us together. Or, rather, we did, but it was only the crude philosophy of survivors. Not that that was anything new. Every single philosophy man has had has been based on the assumption of survival. That way we live to learn from our mistakes. On personal survival. On survival of the species. Sacrificing ourselves to the greater good. All assumed an everlasting future. Means to an end. Not what a moment, an event, an act, a thought is in itself. Survival has been the sole philosophy of our species. Nothing higher."

Herbie opens his mouth to disagree.

"It has, though," Barry Popieluszko insists. "In its simplest form it's been a looking back on bad patches. A Christian, or any religion more or less, says 'God works in mysterious ways'. Because they survived. The surviving optimist says 'See – it all works out in the end'. And the surviving fatalist says 'It must have been meant to be that way'. Because they all got over their bad patch, because things got better for them. While they're in their bad patch, though, they're not so ready to trot out their little aphorisms. Then they're lost, feel deserted, let down in some indefinable way. Even then, though, they know that it'll pass. They assume a continuity of being. Except this time there'll be no survivors. We're going to meet our doom without a coherent philosophy. And that's why there are so many angry people out there. All feel they've been cheated."

"And that makes you happy?"

"Not happy, no. Righteous maybe. Sad too ... So how can I help you?"

Herbie drinks some of his coffee, takes a deep breath. "I'm having trouble finding out about Kate. Her life's got so many closed doors. I was hoping you might be able to open one or two for me."

"Kate was never the communicative one. You've got some idea who killed her, then?"

"Her boyfriend. Her regular boyfriend." Barry grimaces. "And after he killed her he cleared out every trace of himself. Except his prints. And they're not on record. You seen her recently?"

Barry shakes his head.

"How did you split up?" Herbie asks.

"She left me. I was pretty cut up about it at the time. Wouldn't be inexact to say that I married on the rebound."

"And you've got children now?"

"Yes."

Barry finishes his sandwich. "A two and a half year old and a six-month-old. Boys." He looks to the window. "Hope it stops raining for them."

"You got a car?"

"Old red Datsun. Why? MOT expired?"

"Why didn't Kate drive?"

"Had a school friend killed in a car smash. Had a bee in her bonnet about cars. Casual deaths, she called them."

"Was this place always like this?" Herbie indicates the litter of the room.

"Shambles, you mean? Was even worse when Kate was here. Place was knee-deep in empties."

"She lived here with you?"

"Must come as a bit of a shock when you've seen her flat. I thought it might have been that when she left me. So I went and decorated the place from top to bottom. But it wasn't the shambles she left, it was me. Should have seen it coming. But I was drinking pretty heavy at the time. I'd just had my first two books published and didn't know where I was. Neither of them was a success. And after all those years of thinking once I'd been published my every problem would be solved … I was on a self-destructive kick. And Kate stuck with me for most of it. That's why when you say her boyfriend did it," a tightened fist, "it's worse somehow. You see, Kate's one of those women gives herself body and soul to her man. Not that she demeans herself – you can't walk all over her – but once she decides you're her man, that's it. She organises her life to suit you. So long as she believes in what you're doing, her life is subjugated entirely to yours. I suddenly realised what I'd let slip away."

"This is a side of her that's new to me." Herbie swills the coffee around his mug. "I've been to her flat, I've been to her office: she was well-organised, a scientist. I just can't imagine her living here with you."

"She did so for nearly five years. And don't let appearances fool you. In my fashion I am extremely organised. So too Kate in her fashion. Like me, she organises her own little corner of life, no matter what chaos surrounds her. I used to reckon it was a compulsion with her, because she was by nature an untidy person.

She used to say that it was because once she'd got it organised she didn't have to bother her head with it anymore. I'm not so sure it was that simple. She's complicated."

"You met Kate while she was still at college?"

"Post grad. I'm ten years older. Was ten years older."

"I'd have said, from what I know of her so far, that all this is completely out of character. Except that she did have all those art books. You give her any?"

On the walls are several framed paintings.

"Might've done." Barry is searching his mind. "No, can't remember. But there's no contradiction here you know. Science and Art are very compatible. Both, for instance, follow very similar disciplines. In both you work in the dark for years, no real idea where you're going, and at the end of it you've maybe produced something worthwhile. Maybe not. And, scientist or artist, even if you have produced something worthwhile, you may not be able to sell it. Or get any credit for it. That aside, look at Keynes – best economic brain this century, married an opera star. Then you've got Herbert George Wells, the Huxleys, Goethe … I could go on and on. Nor is it such a clear division. These days artists have to be scientists, scientists have to be artists. And another thing – artists, scientists, no matter how good or bad they are, if they take themselves seriously, they are all of them dedicated. All of them in hock to the future. The One Day. Like waiting for a win on the lottery. One Day. And while the work's in progress they're all of them in search of intangibles, indefinables. Like you. You should be able to understand that. The search. How many of your cases do you solve? Fifty percent from what I read. Yet still you go on with them, knowing that half the time they're hopeless. You dig away and dig away and finally emerge with a nugget of truth. Maybe."

"Wouldn't have put it quite like that." Herbie squints. "No, not like that, but I get your drift. You had plenty in common with Kate. Did she drink as well?"

"Not so she got legless. I still don't think you understand quite how much the Arts and Science do have in common. For instance, they share a similar analytical approach. Both rely on observation and experiment. Both know that moment of creation, of blazing clarity, of truth. And both know the difficulty of expressing, in common language, that cryptic truth. And both know the slogging tedium, the endless repetition, the dead ends, the unlikely success of a project ... One difference – mathematics. Mathematics the mother of science, literature the father of art. Yet again, both have to be precise. And language has to express the findings of science. Again Art and Science share the same discipline. So you find artists who dabble in science, and articulate scientists. Hold on a minute," he stands, "while I get my fags."

Herbie drains his now tepid coffee, looks thoughtfully out to the dripping garden. Barry, coming back into the room, follows his gaze.

"Christ I hope it stops raining for them." He sits down. "You got any children?"

"One daughter. Nineteen. Would have been twenty next month. She's taken herself off to Naples."

Barry grunts a smile through the smoke of his cigarette. "Ah, the young, see it all in its stark reality; and react to it with candour. While we ..." he spreads a hand, lets it fall "... we're owned by the habits of a lifetime. We forget we're going to die. Them, they're newly arrived from oblivion. They know what it's like not to exist. To have no identity. Haven't got so much invested in this life as us. Less to lose. Still," he looks back to the window, "I hope it stops raining."

"You're not going to join them?"

Barry Popieluszko determinedly shakes his head. "Know what my next book was to be about? A man acutely aware of the passing of time. Life follows Art. Except this man, so as not to squander a second, ordered and minutely filled his minutes and hours; and lost sight of the years. Years, which when he came to look back, were coloured with no great events, only meticulous monochrome timekeeping. The great events he'd avoided, because a great event would have disrupted his ordered routines, would have impinged on his time-saving. He was never early, never late, always on time. And by saving time he lost it. Not even in his own memory did anything mark the passing of his life. His achievements were small and many, his few failures a minor irritation at the time and soon forgotten. He had aspired to nothing great, only the attainable. No prizes, no forfeits. He had wasted his time in the saving of it. He squirrelled away a minute here, a second there; and then forgot where he'd stored his hoard."

Barry Popieluszko seems about to say more, but drifts into silence. He appears calmer now.

Herbie breaks the silence, "You been to Kate's flat? The one in Victoria?"

"The one with the pink settee? Yeah."

"When was that?"

"Like I said, four years ago. To try to talk her into coming back to me. Matter of fact I laid siege to her. Roses, the works."

"Ever see another man there?"

"No."

"Not once?"

"Was someone in the flat first time I went there. Kate kept me on the doorstep. Told me in future I had to phone beforehand."

"And you did?"

"Yeah, she was all right about it. She wasn't going to quit on five years without some explanations. She even let me sleep with her. Though she made sure I knew that was as far as it went.

Sorry." He stubs out his cigarette. "I find it as difficult to talk about myself as I do to write about myself. My ideas – easy. What happened – it all seems so dull. And there's so much of it."

"Where was the new boyfriend when you were sleeping with her?"

"Gone home for the weekend, I suppose. She told me he was married. So there was no guilt in it for her sleeping with me. That went on for about two months. Until I realised it was going nowhere. Was just a Saturday night screw. It wasn't my life she was concerned with any more. It was somebody else's. I was being fitted into her free time. But she let me down gently. In many ways her leaving did me good. Got me off the bottle and back down to some work. Talking of which …"

Herbie holds up his hand. "Just a couple more minutes. If you don't mind? Kate must have mixed up here with your friends. Any of them keep in touch with her?"

"Not as far as I know."

"Any of them see her with her new boyfriend?"

"I married outside that circle, have lost contact with most of them. Yes." Barry Popieluszko raises a finger. "One of them did see him."

"Name?" Herbie flips open his notebook.

"Gilbert Somebody. I never knew his second name. And I haven't seen him for years. We used to call him The Crumb. He went around picking up the crumbs from other men's tables. A couple'd bust up, Gilbert'd be there on the woman's doorstep. All sympathy and lust. He told one wife he'd come stiff prick in hand to give her back her self-respect. He told me he went round to Kate's flat, said this fat cat came to the door; and poor Gilbert was given the heave-ho."

"Fat cat?"

"Mr Establishment. Cat who gets the cream. City slicker maybe."

"That's him," Herbie says. "Nothing else?"

"Just that." Barry scratches his head. "No. That's it. One fat married cat."

"Was she going out with him before she left you?"

"She was. But I was so wrapped up in myself that I, in time-honoured fashion, was the last to know. Mind you, she was having this trouble with her brother at the time. He was having a nervous breakdown. She was, so she said, going down to Southampton to get him and his wife sorted out. And so she was most of the time. They were in all sorts of a mess. Poor little sod trying to fight free of the influence of his family and only getting more and more wrapped up by them. Kate, of course, didn't see it that way."

"How did you get on with her father?"

"Pompous old git. Thought that anything less than fifty years old was of no consequence. Nothing of importance could be happening in his own time. Wonder what he makes of this?"

"Kate was sorting out her brother?"

"Yes. She was. And from that distance, out of my milieu, she dispassionately judged us. The scales did not come down in my favour. At the same time she met Mr Fat Cat. A man vastly different from my humble self. In a society where money is the only measure of a life mine has been a dismal failure."

"Did Kate tell you anything about him?"

"Only that he was married. And she only told me that when I kept on about her not being wholly committed to him. And, for my self-esteem, she assured me that I didn't know him."

"So what did you talk about when you visited her in her flat?"

"About us of course. About why she'd left me. Where we'd gone wrong. Kate doesn't tell you anything she doesn't want you to know."

"So I've discovered. Think he set her up in the flat?"

"No chance. Not with Kate. Even when she was on a student loan she insisted on paying her whack. She was some woman."

"That I'm coming to believe. You ever meet any of her college friends?"

"Kate never mixed the two. One girl, though, came here once. Wendy, I think."

"Any particular reason Kate moved to Victoria? Seems an odd choice."

"Not that I know of. Maybe she fancied some luxury. She was earning good money. Wanted to indulge herself after the privations of living with me. And now," Barry abruptly stands, "pen and paper beckon."

Herbie reluctantly closes his notebook. "What you writing? More science fiction?"

"End of the universe means the end of the future means the end of science fiction. Means the end of Einstein's Conundrum."

Barry waits while Herbie buttons his damp mac.

"No more worries for this particular hack what sort of society it would have been where, with faster-than-light space travel, you outlived your stay-at-home contemporaries, where you returned home younger than your great grandchildren. That future, tank-de-Lawd, is behind me. Only two words to write now – 'The End'."

"So what're you writing? Fact?"

"Facts alone are not the truth." Barry pauses at the door to the front room. "You should know that. You must have stood in the witness box, sworn to tell the truth, and told true facts. Those facts though weren't the whole truth. No. Truth is more often fiction than fact. So what I'm writing today is a sort of history of the world. Explaining it to myself. A lament. And now," a grimace, "I've got Kate to add to it."

Herbie fumbles inside his mac for his notepad, scribbles on it, tears off the page. "If you think of anything that might help me find Kate's murderer, night or day, give me a ring on either of these two numbers. Something's staring me in the face and I can't see it."

"Know the feeling well." Barry takes the piece of paper. "Know what I've been trying to describe all morning? – heat lines in water. Writhing like invisible clouds. Yet visible? It's bugged me for years, that description. Like frail spider's webs turning and breaking, and reforming in a persistent breeze. Wet webs? By gawd it's not easy."

Barry follows Herbie to the door, smiling, studies him. "Bet you're not popular with the people you work with."

"What makes you say that?"

"Bet you're not."

"I'm not playmate of the month, if that's what you mean."

"Knew it." Barry grins. "You enjoy your job. You're probably good at it, and the work is all-important to you. You're a maverick to all those safe institutionalised people."

"I'm not exactly known as a barrel of laughs. Hardly call myself a maverick, though."

"We two must be among the lucky few."

"How's that?" Herbie turns his mac collar up.

"At the end of the world we've got problems to solve, things to do."

'The past is an invention of the moment.'
        Barry Popieluszko. Happy Robot Goes Cosmic: Fire Dragon.

Thursday: 16:03

Herbie reaches over his desk, picks up the phone, "Watkins."

"Detective Inspector Watkins?" A woman's voice, London accent.

"Speaking."

"Still Inspector is it? Thought it'd be Superintendent at least by now."

"Who is this?"

"Two days to go, Inspector. How's it feel?"

"What do you want?"

"Might've known you'd still be working. What poor bastard you hounding this time? Still, can't get him twenty years, can you? Not that it makes any difference. Not now. Come Saturday we'll all be going. You and him. Know how it feels now, do you? Want to know how I feel? You fascist bastard. Filth that's what you are. Good name for you. You …"

Herbie returns the phone to its cradle.

'Look back on those jobs you've had, which you did solely for the wage, lived for the weekends ... Ask yourself now how many weeks of your life you wished away?'

Barry Popieluszko. Psychotic Android Eats: Fire Dragon.

Thursday: 17:17

"You're early." Sal is standing at the sink.

From behind Herbie slips his arms around her waist, hugs her to him. "What's cooking?" He drops his chin on her shoulder.

"Roast." She scrubs, jerking him, at a pan. "Thought we'd have it today in case we don't make Sunday."

"Could end up having two roasts." He makes kissing noises in her ear.

"If you think I'm cooking two roasts in one week," she steps out of his arms and over to the cooker, "you've got another think coming. You're only getting roast today because I've been home since twelve."

Her voice lost its bantering lightness on her last words.

"Works have closed. Wasn't enough in today to man the line. No workers," her smile is fatalistic, "no canteen."

"Wondered how long it'd be." Herbie begins taking off his jacket. "So what're you going to do with yourself tomorrow?"

"Got it all planned." She turns the gas down under a pan. "I'm going to clean this house from top to bottom."

Herbie pauses to look at her happy self, frowns. "Bit pointless?" He hangs his jacket over the back of a chair, loosens his tie.

"Not really," she says, looking into a pan. "I thought about it today ..."

Herbie watches the tip of her nose move as she talks about cleaning and decorating, recalls his conversation with Liz Bradley, thinks of clever Kate Soames, listens to Sal; going on about a soap powder advert, obvious message behind it, and he wants to shout at her – I don't give a shit! Not one single solitary shit what you think of a stupid fucking advert!

Knows he won't. Can't.

He and Sal don't argue. Has become chapter and verse of their marriage. Though they used to, before the operation on her ovaries. She'd been monthly bitter then. And, accommodating man that he is, Herbie had almost learnt to live with that, to bite down most times on his anger. Or use any excuse to stay away from home, which excuses she had saved up against him, for the next month.

Then had come the almost too late diagnosis of cancer. Julie was two. His horror at watching Sal, the plaything of doctors, as she lost weight and hair, looking down at tiny trusting little Julie and not knowing what to do with her, with his life, if ... He can still recall his private groaning desolation at almost losing her; followed by his bewilderment at the two years mute depression which followed Sal's physical recovery.

Julie knows of the illness; but not the depth of it. Julie sees the coping mechanisms as her mother's character, as her mother's chosen way of life. Only Herbie knows how close to the surface Sal has been since, knows that if she once dips, she sinks. Herbie has adapted himself to that fragility, that rigidity, the keeping of a certain kind of order to keep thinking at bay, the carefully lacquered hair mimicking the wigs she once had to wear.

It is in his power to destroy her. He can't, has to let her cope with this latest of life's disasters to come her way.

"… So I thought about it today. About how you don't notice where you live until you've just cleaned it. Or decorated it. I decided it's homemaking we love more than the home itself. And that's how they manage to flog us all that gear for our houses." She comes to him, hugs him, kisses him. "Clever, eh?"

"You or them?" Herbie kisses her nose.

"Them first. Now me."

"What about Saturday? Don't look like there'll be any shops open."

"Hardly seems any point shopping if we're not going to be here next week. And that looks pretty certain now. Thought I'd pop over and see Mum. You needn't come if you don't want."

"Why's it so certain now?"

"They had the Minister of Environment on telly lunchtime. He's resigned. Said that the Prime Minister's known about it since last week, but the Cabinet chose to do and say nothing."

Herbie holds her from him. "So what," he speaks slowly, "is he doing on the telly?"

"Said he felt the public had a right to know." She releases herself, bends to the oven. "Load of waffle about someone having the courage to give the public the unpalatable news."

"The bastard! The snivelling little bastard!" Herbie grabs his jacket up in his fist.

Sal stares up at him, surprised by his anger.

"Do you know what damage he's done?" he asks her, her incomprehension feeding his anger. (He has surprised himself at his outburst, but does not now want to stop.)

Very slowly Sal straightens. "He just said he wanted it on record …"

"Record! What bloody record? There'll be no soddin' records in three days time. Little toe rag!" Herbie furiously flings his jacket onto the floor.

"He just said," Sal shrugs, "that he couldn't stand silently by while the country collapsed around him. I can see his ..."

"Don't you realise what he's done?" Herbie looks away, turns back to her bewilderment. "That's a hooligan's bloody charter he's just come up with. There'll be nothing now. Nothing! Anyone with a bit of savvy could see that the government was saying nothing because there was nothing they could bloody say. And now that snivelling little twat's scoring points at the end of the world. Just how long has this prince of discretion managed to keep his big trap shut?"

"Since Monday, he said. Monday morning." Sal is trying to restrain her tears. "He said they'd all been asked not to say anything. But in light of recent events ..."

"Can't lose, can he?" Herbie leans forward to shout at her. "No one's going to boot him out of his job. No. Because the world ends in three days' time. And no one's going to deny it, because they can't. So for three days he's going to be the media's bloody darling. A three day hero! Toe rag!"

"Herbie?"

"Do you know the damage that snivelling little squirt's done? Do you?" Herbie asks of her. "Let me tell you the damage he's done. Just one example." Herbie thrusts his finger at her. "Mike's been in every day this week. The only one bar me. Even Jim didn't turn in today. And do you know why Mike's been in? Because he's been waiting for someone to tell him the newspapers have got it wrong. Just sat there in his office waiting for the phone to ring. Tomorrow he's not going to be there. Not now. Because of that irresponsible creep!" He gestures towards the living room and the telly.

"I thought you didn't like Mike?"

"I don't. He's another prize creep. But while he was coming in he could have been of some use. Now? Now it's just bloody Jack Todd here. And not only that. It's all the people like Mike, the people who didn't know what else to do – so they went to work. They kept a few buses, a few trains running. A few shops open ..."

.Frustrated by her continuing incomprehension Herbie turns full circle. "You know that most of the hospitals have closed? I got a memo about it this morning. The only one there. The only memo. Christ knows where it came from. Hospitals closed except for life or death operations. But mostly they're dishing out painkillers. Tell me who's going to be dishing out painkillers tomorrow? Nobody. Tomorrow there'll be nothing. Not now that snotty little twat's shot off his mouth. He's taken their last prop away." Herbie kicks at his jacket, glares at it wrapped around the table leg.

Sal cautiously approaches him, lays a hand on his arm. "You one of those men, Herbie?"

"No!" he throws off her hand, steps past her, spins around, "I knew it was true the second I saw they hadn't denied it. And I know exactly what I want to do. I want to collar the nasty bastard who beat Katherine Helen Soames to death. That's what I want to do. And that little toe rag's made it nigh on bloody impossible now."

"Is it that important Herbie?" Sal holds a tissue to her nose. "I've never seen you so angry before."

"And I've never seen you cry so much before."

Stooping to her tissue, Sal stumbles out of the kitchen, slams the door behind her. Herbie listens to her clumping up the stairs.

"Ah shit," he says.

Bending to the floor Herbie picks up his jacket. "Shit shit shit." He shakes the jacket out, dusts it with the flat of his hand, hangs it back over the chair.

He stays there a moment, his hands resting on the chair, then he takes a deep breath, walks slowly to the door.

"Sal," he calls up the stairs. "Sorry, love. Not your fault."

'I am a witness. My function in life is to bear witness.'
        Barry Popieluszko. Happy Robot Goes Cosmic: Fire Dragon.

Thursday: 23:44

Herbie picks up the phone, "Watkins."

"Daddy?"

"Julie?"

"First time lucky!" she laughs, surprised.

Sal is hurriedly getting up from the game of scrabble.

"Where are you?" Herbie asks Julie.

"In a little place, sort of cafe, just this side of Lyons. We were going to go through Switzerland, but a lorry driver on the ferry told us they'd closed the border. So we're going through the Frejus tunnel tomorrow."

"Did you travel all night?"

"When we weren't on the ferry. But we stopped for a long lunch. Had it outside."

"You're making good time."

"Looks like we may have got the last ferry over too. The French crew said they were going home. Dad?"

"Yes?"

"Dad, Dijon was burning. The whole city. There were people on fire jumping in the river. I can't believe I've seen it."

The voice is on the verge of tears.

"It's all right where you are now?"

"There's a wood here. We're going to sleep there."

132

"How's Peter?"

"Soon as he saw the flames he stopped. They were going mad. They were even turning over ambulances."

She is silent.

"Julie?"

"Sorry. I wasn't going to tell you. Didn't want to worry you."

"You're all right?"

"Yes. We had to make a detour, though. Got lost a couple of times."

Sal is making frantic signals to be given the phone.

"Here's your Mum."

Sal jams the phone to her ear. "Julie? Hello love ... No, it's all right. We decided to wait up anyway. Just in case. We're playing scrabble ... Oh he keeps coming out with these clever bloody words ... How's Peter? ... Good ... Good ... Really? ... Mind you don't get saddlesore." Sal gives her canteen laugh.

Herbie gestures to Sal to let him have the phone back.

"Did you say you had a tent?" Sal asks. "No ... Still, you did the right thing, love: been tipping it down here all day ... How're you managing for food? ... Did he? ... Quite right. Sounds like you're in safe hands then, love ... Oh all right then, love. Bye. take care, darling. Quick," she shoves the phone at Herbie, "she's running out of change."

"Julie?"

"Dad?"

"Tell Peter to get plenty of rest. You need all your wits about you on a bike. No point in pushing himself too hard and having an accident now. You tell him."

"He's listening, told me to tell you not to worry, Dad, he's not going to take any chances. I won't let him."

"How're you managing for petrol? Places open?"

"We got a spare can. It's pretty good on ..."

The line clicks and bleeps.

'Looking death in the face when you're young is a gesture. (Fatal sometimes, thrilling too, daring all. Except that the young expect to live forever.) Looking death in the face when you're old is neither frightening nor thrilling; it's your only future.'

Barry Popieluszko. Happy Robot Goes Cosmic: Fire Dragon.

Friday: 08:56

In their corner of the office Jim is emptying ashtrays into wastepaper bins, collecting up plastic coffee cups.

"Morning." Herbie takes off his mac, shakes it. "Didn't think I'd be seeing you again."

"Yeah. Well." Jim wipes around an ashtray with a screwed-up newspaper, returns the ashtray to a desktop.

"Sorry about that."

"Don't worry about it." Herbie hangs up his mac. "The world's gone stark staring bloody mad. You'd be an odd man if it hadn't touched you."

"Touched is the word."

"I even lost my temper with Sal yesterday." Herbie sits down. "First time ever. Our first real row. Nothing much really. Had to spend the whole evening making up though. Still, cleared the air. Was all a bit unnatural before. Carrying on as if nothing was happening."

"We got anything on?" Jim stamps down the rubbish in a wastepaper bin. His shoes have been shined.

"Katherine Helen Soames still. You back to work then?"

134

Jim sits behind his tidied desk. "I wanted to be somewhere where I was of some use." He moves the telephone. "No one else in?"

"Just you and me. Maybe the boss."

"He's not. Unless he's coming in later."

"Doubt it. See the news last night?"

"Environment Minister you mean? Saw it in the papers. Squealing little runt."

Herbie lays his notebook open on the desk, looks back through the pages. "You find out anything at the college?"

"Did I ever?" Jim grunts. "That's what led to me not turning in yesterday. All those fuckin' college types asking me what was the point. What's the point? And outside in the street there's bloody riots going on and no one doing a thing to stop it. So I thought, where's the sense in it all? In all that we've done? Our Miss Soames, methinks, is well out of it. Her boyfriend, did he but know it, has done her a big favour. So why am I bothering looking for him?"

Jim spreads his arms apologetically. "All things thus considered, I adjourned for a drink, and thought about it all. And it wasn't until then that I realised how much, just in our ordinary lives, the future governs us. I started thinking back to all those tomorrows I'd worried about. Why'd I bothered? What had been the point? Talk about frustrating. Bloody frustrating. Because what was the point in being angry? Anger comes from frustration. Frustration comes from being stopped from doing what you want to do. I got no future to do anything in. So I couldn't be angry. Because what could I be angry against? The end of the world? Told you it was frustrating. And the more I drank the less sense it made."

Jim slowly shakes his head. "The papers are having this feud, you know? Each one's claiming it was their astrologer who predicted the end of the world first. So I had another drink. Turned into a bender."

"And you ran out of drink?"

"No way. Nobody's paying for booze now. They're just busting the pubs wide open and helping themselves. Party to end all parties. Single people. People who want to be single. You're all right, you got Sal and Julie. The rest of us, though, we got to go out, find someone's ear we can bend."

"Julie's gone to Naples."

"On her tod?"

"Some boy from college. Peter. On his motorbike. He's all right, though. Sensible. Soon as he saw the state France was in he stocked up with food. Julie phoned last night, told Sal they got so many French loaves their bike looks like a hedgehog on two wheels."

Herbie toys with his notebook. "Dijon was on fire she said. They're hoping to get into Italy today."

He looks up to Jim. "So what happened to bring you back? Run out of ears to bend? Or you come back to bend mine?"

"No. I'll tell you how it happened, though. I was in this pub in Kilburn. Don't ask me why Kilburn. Anyway I was sitting in the bog. Paralytic. Graffiti all over the walls. And I was too pissed to read any of it. Except somebody had written something under the bog roll. I could just see the last few letters. Anyway, after looking at it for half 'n hour, I just had to see what it said. So I lifted up the bog roll. Know what it said?"

"You're going to tell me."

"It said, 'Don't look upon it as the end of the world, see it more as a cure for the common cold.'"

Herbie laughs.

"And that," Jim says, "sort of put it in perspective. I reckon that bloke ought to be paid to go round London and write that under every bog roll."

"And you're definitely back to work?" Herbie asks him.

"Looks like it. Though don't ask me why."

"Maybe," Herbie winks at him, "we're a couple of idealists"

"Never been accused of that before."

Herbie has gone back to toying with his notebook. Jim opens and closes a desk drawer. "So how far we got with Miss Soames?"

"I found him." Herbie signifies the photograph on the noticeboard. "One Barry Popieluszko. She lived with him until four years ago. A writer. Camden. He's married now, two kids, hasn't really seen her since. Full stop."

"Where do we go from here?"

"Any mention of a girl called Barbara at the college?"

"I told you – no mention of nobody."

"Well … There's still the picture. The lilies. If you could go back there: he should be back from Wales by now. Got the address?"

Jim flips open his notebook. "Yeah. Islington. What about the stake-out?"

"Went by there yesterday. Place is shut down. No one in their right mind's going to be robbing that."

"What're you going to be doing?"

"Thought I'd have another go at Mrs Harris first. See if I can't get something more out of her. And from there I'll probably be going on to Chiswick."

Herbie flips his notebook shut. "Something's staring me in the face and I can't see it. If I get nowhere this morning we'll meet back here for lunch. If we can get any. Forgot me sandwiches this morning. And we'll take it from there."

"We got cars?"

"Yeah. Why?"

"We got petrol, then?"

"So far as I know. No one else here is using it."

"You know all the garages are closed? Cars run out of petrol they dump 'em where they stall. Fast lane even. Which is why there's so many pile-ups."

"No problem for us so far as I know. Better check first."

"Right." Jim stands, pockets his notebook. "And if anybody asks me what's the point today I'll tell 'em I'm an idealist."

'The present, the here and now, is always flawed.'
  Barry Popieluszko. Happy Robot Goes Cosmic: Fire Dragon.

Friday: 09:51

Herbie breaks the seal on the door to number twenty-three.

The flat is as he left it. Save for two dirty coffee cups beside the kitchen sink.

In the other rooms he pauses to touch various items, comes to a stop in the living room, staring down on the shattered telephone, its thin blue and white wires like scrawny intestines, its plastic splinters like bone shards. He crouches to the records and CDs – Verdi, Puccini, Britten. He turns to the slewed pile of art books – da Vinci, Michelangelo, David …

He flips through her quote book. No quotes attributed to Barry Popieluszko. 'He saw the odd in everything, and missed the even.' T E Lawrence. Herbie has known detectives like that, always looking for the clever answer when the simple has been staring them in the face. The rest of the quotes are as impersonal, will get him nowhere.

He tosses the pad onto the desk's untidy heap. Every single thing here had its place in her life. He knows her now: a woman who was often alone. Abruptly he leaves the flat.

'Only animals belong in the reactive here and now, are creatures solely of touch, sense and fear. Human beings belong in worlds of the mind, to hierarchies within hierarchies, what they do governed by what they think their peers might think of their doing it.'

Barry Popieluszko. The Watcher: Kerala Books.

Friday: 10:13

Mrs Harris opens the door to number twenty-two. "Never expected to see you again." She seems pleased that he has called. "Thought you'd have gone off for a holiday. Everyone else has, they say."

"Like to finish what I've started."

"Come in." She shuffles aside.

"Thanks." Out of habit Herbie ducks his head as he steps over the threshold.

Herbie goes ahead of her into the living room. A Yorkshire terrier, blue ribbon round its neck, jumps off an armchair.

"You must be Jason." Herbie squats to the small dog, encircles its whole body in his hand.

"Sit down. Sit down," Mrs Harris tells Herbie. "Sit down. I'd offer you a cup of tea, but I don't have a drop of milk in the place."

"That's all right." Herbie plants himself on the sofa, releases the small panting dog. "I can't really stop long. Just dropped by to see if you've thought of anything."

"Anything?"

"Anything that might help us catch our nasty friend from next door."

"Oh, I'm sorry." Mrs Harris lifts the dog onto her lap. "I haven't given it much thought. What with all the other news. I didn't think you'd be bothering now."

"News doesn't seem to have upset you much?"

"I know. I know. Makes me feel quite guilty. To be perfectly honest, I'm relieved in a way. You see I was quite worried – about when I was going to die. Because if I went before Jason I was worried who would take care of him after I'd gone. And I was worried what would happen to me if he went before me. He's eleven now, you know. Old for a small dog. It's an awful thing to say, but I feel as if I've outlived everybody. My son was killed, you know. Fell out of a tree. He was only ten. Then there was my brother, then Jack. I've been all on my own, except for Jason, for years you see. But now my worries are over. Jason and I will be going together."

She pets the dog. Herbie sits smiling at her.

"I don't know how I can help you," she says.

"This man you saw her with. Where was it?"

"He came out of her flat. I think I was waiting for the lift. I might've been taking in the milk."

"You said you saw her with him."

"Did I? Yes I did. That was another time. They came out of the lift. She said hello."

"He didn't say anything?"

"No."

"A businessman, you reckon. Why a businessman?"

"He looked like one. Had on a suit. You don't see many suits these days."

"But why a businessman? I've got a suit on. Why not a policeman? Or a doctor, for instance?"

"No." Mrs Harris thinks. "No, doctors look different. They wear tweeds, don't they? Some look a bit scruffy. Maybe it's just because they're tired. No, he was smart. Smart and expensive."

"Couldn't have been a salesman?"

"No … No, they've got a look about them. You know – pushy, sly. No, he looked like what I'd call well-set-up."

"When was it you saw him?"

"Oh, months ago."

"I mean was it a weekday evening, or a weekend?"

"It would've been a weekday. Definitely a weekday. Sundays the block's practically empty. And on Saturdays you see I always take Jason out early. They have parties here on Saturdays. I got caught in the lift once. Not that they meant any harm, just a bit too lively for old bones like mine."

"You would recognise him if you saw him again?"

"Oh yes. I was as close to him as I am to you now."

Herbie pulls out the photograph of Barry Popieluszko, holds it up before her, "Recognise him?"

"No." She tilts her head to study it from another angle. "I'll get my glasses."

She hands the dog to Herbie. The excited terrier pants into his face, tries to plant his licks on Herbie's face. The tiny heartbeat is like a clock ticking fast inside Herbie's big hand.

Mrs Harris has studied the photograph, swaps it for the dog. "Wouldn't have said he was her type at all."

"This man you saw …" Herbie returns the photograph to his pocket, "nothing else you remember about him? Any small thing?"

"I'm sorry. No." Wetting her little finger she rubs it over the dog's tiny black nose. "No. Only wish I could help. Must be very frustrating."

"Can say that again." Herbie tiredly pushes himself to his feet. "Thanks for your time, Mrs Harris."

'If here is where we've reached using one map, and here is wrong, we get a new map, not a new route to here on the old map.'
Barry Popieluszko. Psychotic Android Eats: Fire Dragon.

Friday: 11:14

Mr Trellpott is in the workshop, bent to the open rear of a laminated metal box. Room smells of hot metal, burnt chemicals. Offices upstairs are all empty.

"Was hoping I'd find you here." Herbie announces his presence.

Mr Trellpott extricates himself from the back of the box, recognises Herbie, smiles pleasantly at him. Today Mr Trellpott is wearing gold-rimmed glasses. "Another half hour, you wouldn't have. I'm only here now," he lays down a soldering spike, "because I've been boasting for years that I'd build my eldest son a customised robot. Deadlines always got in the way. Now," like a show compère he holds out his hand, "meet Super-Rob."

The metal box has spindly arms and legs. The face is a screen, a small array of buttons beneath it. The legs end in a pair of rollerboots.

Assuming Herbie's appraisal to be critical Mr Trellpott hastens to explain, "It's meant to look amateurish. Children prefer it. They like to see some moving parts. Makes it more approachable."

"Looks fun," Herbie says. "But won't it," he hesitates to point out the obvious, "fall over when it moves?"

"Got gyros in here." Mr Trellpott bends again to the back of it. "Boots are power-driven. Air brakes. Audio-responsive. All the very latest. Nothing but the best." He emerges from the box. "If three years late."

"How's it powered?" Herbie thinks it an intelligent question.

"Dry cells. Rechargeable. What brings you here?"

"Same as last time. Our Katherine Helen Soames. And no further along. I have to admit I'm getting desperate."

"Got to admire," Mr Trellpott, grunting, straightens his back, "your persistence. Anything at all I can do to help. Though I must confess, in light of our imminent departure, I haven't given Kate much thought."

"No idea who her current boyfriend might have been?"

"None. Sorry. No ideas whatsoever."

"What was she working on four years ago? What companies was she dealing with?"

"Four years ago? No idea offhand. But we've got it all upstairs. I'll come up with you in a minute. Just a couple more minor refinements." Mr Trellpott pushes up his glasses, puts his head again into the back of the box. "If you don't mind, that is."

"Go ahead." Herbie says, looks around for somewhere to sit. He hoists himself up onto a workbench.

Mr Trellpott hums to himself. Picking up a set of steel callipers, Herbie measures his thumb. Inside the box Mr Trellpott, for a moment, breaks into song. Herbie smiles. "You seem much happier than when I last saw you."

"Wasn't a good day." Mr Trellpott says from within the box. "And the news you brought didn't help. But," he pauses as he does something, "I wouldn't be much of a scientist, or a businessman, if I couldn't face facts. The fact is I've accepted it."

His hand reaches blindly out for the soldering spike, finds it. "That we created, that we were responsible – that was the illusion." He replaces the soldering spike. "This week I've come to see that, though I've not achieved what I set out to do, what I have done is no small thing. Do you know that this city is running at this moment only because of people like me?"

He steps back from the box, wipes both his hands on the seat of his trousers. "Without people like me," he taps himself on the chest, "without our inventions, without our many innovations, this city would now be a complete and utter shambles. But, because of people like me, your sewage works continue to function, as does your street lighting, your traffic lights, your telephones, your water, your gas and electricity. Even your televisions. And your newspapers. No small achievement, that."

Mr Trellpott disappears again into the box. "So many people worse off than me," he says. "I was talking to an old naturalist friend of mine. Devoted his life to saving species from extinction. Risked his own life at times. Only to find now that he needn't have bothered."

"Hadn't thought of that," Herbie says. "I know it's not the same, but I keep thinking of my mother and father. Both dead now. Somehow, though, don't ask me why, I feel they've been cheated by all this."

"Mind you," Mr Trellpott says, "who says we've got to find reasons for doing what we want to do?"

"People keep asking me for a reason."

"Maybe there aren't any."

"I've spent most of my life looking for them."

"Don't seem to have been many. Do there?"

"True."

"Things happen," Mr Trellpott says. "Afterwards we try to find out how and why. Put a name to it. So we can justify ourselves in the future. Now there's no afterwards."

Herbie shifts on the bench, uncomfortable with the vagueness of the conversation. "You said Kate worked late sometimes. Any times in particular when she couldn't work?"

"No. Not that I can think of. Actually no, there wasn't any time she wouldn't work. The rest would complain if they had to stay late too often. Husbands and wives off-stage grumbling to them. Kate never."

"Pity."

"Have you thought …?" Mr Trellpott rests his thin forearms on the box. "You're looking for a man, you say. Are you sure the murderer couldn't have been a woman?"

"What makes you say that?"

"I'm not saying it was Liz, but she and Kate were very friendly."

"Lesbian, you mean?"

"None of my business, but I sometimes got that impression. Liz was very possessive, protective about Kate."

"No." Herbie shakes his head. "Kate had sex with her assailant shortly before he killed her. Forensic points to it being a man."

"What if the woman, jealous, came in just afterwards?"

"A possibility. I'll have a look at forensic again. No. It's pure supposition. Why would a girlfriend clear out all evidence of a boyfriend?"

"Or of herself. Muddy the waters?"

"Either way we've still got to find the man who had sex with her. I take it that Liz Bradley was here Monday afternoon?"

"She was. And very bolshie that day too. But what I'm saying is that it could have been another girlfriend."

"It's a thought."

"Only one I can come up with."

Mr Trellpott lays aside his tools, takes one last look at the box's innards, lifts it around so the blank screen is facing Herbie.

"Moment of truth," he tells Herbie. "When I power him on, say 'Hello Super-Rob.'"

Mr Trellpott's long fingers press switches in the back of the box. The box and its limbs stir slightly, adjust its balance. The screen crackles, settles into a lime green face, straight red mouth, two black curving eyelids. Mr Trellpott nods to Herbie.

In his best constable-dealing-with-a-member-of-the-public-voice Herbie addresses the screen. "Hello, Super-Rob."

The straight red mouth curls into a smile and the black eyelids slowly lift to reveal two aquamarine eyes.

"Hello Paul," Super-Rob says, the red lips parting. He has an American accent.

"My son's name," Mr Trellpott whispers. "Tell him to do something. Say Super-Rob first."

"Super-Rob," Herbie says, "turn around."

"Whatever you say." The robot inclines his feet, turns completely around. Mr Trellpott glances at his watch,

"That'll do." He leans behind to flick switches inside the robot, takes off his glasses. "Let's go and have a look at those files. Four years ago, you say?"

'To think on all the times one could have died and didn't die is to come by the delusion that one's life means something.'

Barry Popieluszko. Psychotic Android Eats: Fire Dragon.

'People who look back to the past, who take all their reference points from the past, end up walking into walls.'

Barry Popieluszko. The Watcher: Kerala Books.

Friday: 13:20

Herbie sits at his desk, arms behind his head, staring at the two photographs on the noticeboard. (He has moved the noticeboard to directly in front of his desk.) Spread out on the desk before him are his notebook, the few pages of the post mortem, the forensic report, the list of tailors, the three London tailors' lists of their customers; the names and addresses of the painters from the foyer, the men working on the site in Bethnal Green, the staff list from CAS Ltd.

If Herbie had the men … If he had the time … he would by now have amassed reams of information directly and indirectly concerned with Katherine Helen Soames and her murderer. A few common factors would by now have emerged from that disparate information. One name on more than one list would by now have led his hand towards the collar of her homicidal lover. He would at least have had one definite suspect. But the few names he had, on the few lists he had, were all unconnected. Meaningless abstracts.

Letting his arms drop he reaches forward to the telephone, taps the number.

"Yes?"

"Liz Bradley?"

"Yes?"

"Detective Inspector Watkins here."

"Hello Inspector. Still hot on the trail?" She sounds cheerful.

"On the trail, yes. Hot, no."

"What can I do for you? Only I was just about to go out."

"I was wondering if you'd thought anymore about Kate? If you might now have any idea who killed her?"

"'Fraid not, Inspector. To tell the truth, I've re-discovered tennis. Me and a girl upstairs. And no sooner do we discover a mutual love of the game than it pisses down. I don't know if you've noticed, Inspector, but it's just stopped."

"I'll try not to keep you. Can you think back four years to when Kate moved house. Did she give any indication who her new boyfriend might be?"

"Sorry. No."

"I've got a list here of the jobs she was working on at the time she moved. Do you think someone connected with one of those jobs could have been her new boyfriend?"

"Could have been."

"There's a Mr Willis, Barfait, Darboy. Names mean anything to you?"

"Sorry."

"Gresham?"

"No."

"She ever talk about going to Preston, Lancashire?"

"Not as far as I can remember. Is that where he is?"

"Gresham yes. The other three are Londoners. And not one of them lives anywhere near Victoria."

"Couldn't have been someone working for them?"

149

"I can't get hold of any of them. Two don't answer their phones, two got answering machines. Did she say why she was moving to Victoria?"

"No. Just that she'd got a new flat. No reasons for it. Just about furniture."

"Nothing else?"

"She might well have gone to Preston. Must have if we had a job there. More often than not she was out on site. All over the country. Europe too. It was her job."

"Nothing specific you can remember? Something out of the ordinary? Anything?"

"I'm sorry, Inspector. I ..."

"You said that Kate couldn't make opera in the week. Only Fridays and Saturdays. She ever give a reason?"

"No. And I never asked."

"But she could fit in your holidays without any trouble?"

"Yes."

"In the summer?"

"Yes."

"The name Barry Popieluszko ring any bells?"

"Sorry, no."

"He's a writer."

"Is he? I don't read much. Unless I have to. I only wish I could be of some help. But honestly that's all I know."

"Was Kate a homosexual?"

"What!?"

·"Well, she had no visible boyfriend, she went on holidays with just you, and the only friend she ever brought to dinner was an old college friend – female. Did she ever make any advances to you?"

"Good God, no. Who put that idea into your head?"

"Like I said, I'm getting desperate."

"Indeed you are."

"Sorry to have bothered you."

"Oh, don't apologise, Inspector. I wish you the best of luck."

"I need it. Have a good game."

"I've been practising my serve indoors. Broke a window. No stopping me now. Must go, Inspector. Good luck."

"Thanks."

Herbie presses down the receiver, releases it, taps Barry Popieluszko's number.

As before, there is no answer.

'Born from nothing, we live in obscure times, disappear into a nameless obscurity.'

Barry Popieluszko. Raw As Birth: White Swan.

Friday 13:31

At a shouting outside on the stairwell, Herbie takes his hands from behind his head, is sitting forward when the outer office door is banged open. A bellowing, louder now, of garbled curses. Herbie recognises Mike's voice in the shout.

Kicking open the inner doors Mike comes, with exaggerated movements, to a standstill – striped tie and dark suit askew – inside the large office. Face red and wet shiny with tears and snot, he glares across at Herbie.

"Fuck it!" he shouts at Herbie. Leans forward from the hips to shout again, "Fuck it Fuck it Fuck it!"

Mike's hands are now on the desk top. As trained, Herbie lowers his eyes to Mike's chest: avoid eye-contact with the psychotic (eye-contact will invite challenge) while keeping eyes centred on the chest – this will give awareness of potentially threatening body movement.

Mike's movement is to swivel, grab the back of a chair and, screaming, bring it down hard on the corner angle of the nearest desk. Except that the chair, being of tubular metal and moulded plastic, springs up out of Mike's hands, bouncing straight into his face. Like waving away midges Mike flaps his arms around and the chair goes tumbling away across the office.

Herbie waits while Mike glares at him.

"Still here, then. Still playing at policemen."

Herbie keeps his eyes on the round chest, doesn't look up even when Mike bows over a sob. (As with other manic episodes Herbie has witnessed, this too, being exaggerated, appearing histrionic, seems superficially false. Herbie though does not doubt the hectic pace of the mind that creates this appearance, nor its dangers.)

Mike shudders a breath. Tears are dripping from him. Wailing, he puts back his head and flailing his arms goes walking stiff-legged around the office, behind the noticeboard, out the other side. "No!" he shouts. "No!" Picking up another chair he comes stumbling across to Herbie, who pushes himself back from his desk and to his feet as the chair comes crashing down. One metal leg smashes through the telephone, both handset and dial.

Still Herbie avoids eye-contact, looks at Mike's chest, tie askew. Mike is shaking his lowered head.

The plastic of this chair has broken. When Mike goes to raise it, again, above his head bits of it swing loose into his face. He shakes it, growling like an infuriated dog, throws a bit of it at the noticeboard, a bit at the nearest window. The iron and plastic rebound off the double-glazing.

"Ah, fuck it." There is the laughter of despair inside the words. "Fuck it. Fuck it." Mike, almost casually, throws the rest of the chair bits at Herbie. Herbie ducks to one side, then the other. There are no more chair bits to throw. The pieces of the shattered phone are all connected by bits of blue, white and red wire.

"Bollocks to it," Mike says. Walking away he cries out, "Why? Fucking why?"

He runs, part-stumbling towards the door, stops and walks through it. Herbie hears the second door bump closed, slowly follows to hear Mike, down in the echoing stairwell, shouting, "No No No No No …"

'We seek, in all that we do, a continuance. Others may enter and leave our small world, but our small world goes on – house, street, workplace, family. Others enter by marriage, are born, are accommodated. They leave, they die, are buried outside and the circle is closed... In reality there are no sentimental continuances. Death, discontinuance, is in us all.'

Barry Popieluszko. The Watcher: Kerala Books.

Friday: 14:31

Jim, red in the face, comes bumping through the office lugging two lumpy carrier bags.

"Well?" Herbie greets him.

"Been all over bloody London. Found a little shop back of Fleet Street, come the end."

Groaning, Jim dumps the carrier bags on a desk. "Even got a couple bottles of whisky. Mind you, that little lot cost me nigh on a week's wages." He notices the pile of broken bits of chair and phone that Herbie, while waiting, has collected up onto one desk. "What happened here?"

"Mike paid us a visit. Completely lost it. You didn't see him on your way in?"

Jim shakes his head. Herbie has plugged one of the other phones into the socket near his desk, nervously tests it again. "Get anywhere with the picture?"

"Blank. He was there but couldn't remember who he sold it to." Jim has begun to unpack one of the carrier bags. "Years ago, he said. Then I showed him the picture of Barry Whatsisname. He knows him, used to hang around with him. Said it might've been him he sold it to. I had to interview them in the nude."

"You had to strip?"

"No, they were nude. And their kids. Said they were going naked to the end of the world. Wasn't a pretty sight."

Whatever Jim is looking for is not in the first carrier. "Funny what clothes hide." He starts unpacking the second carrier. "Quite fancied her last time I saw her. She's still all right from the neck up. And that's where I kept looking. How'd you get on?"

"Nowhere. Just going over the same ground."

"Nothing?"

"Not a thing. What've we got?"

"Two rounds of ham was all that was going." Jim finds them, "And that's got to be the most expensive sandwich you've ever eaten." He drops the packaged sandwich on Herbie's desk. "I couldn't believe it when I found the shop. Like a little plate glass oasis. Practically everywhere else's been looted. Said he'd been guarding it. Got like this Stone Age club with a nail through the end of it."

Herbie pulls apart the packaging. "I meant," he says, "let's see where we've got with Katherine Helen Soames."

"Oh, right." Jim sits behind his desk, gets up to move the noticeboard so he can see Herbie. Sitting back down he takes a bite of his sandwich.

"She lived alone," Herbie says, "had a regular boyfriend of four years' standing. On Monday he took it into his head to kill her."

"We're sure it's him?" Jim moves some of the shopping aside the better to see Herbie.

"Not a whisper of anyone else. Unless she was a lesbian."

"Lesbian?" Jim smiles. "She had sex with a man. Lesbians don't have semen. Unless she had some new kind of dildo, shoots out O positive spunk."

"Girlfriend could have come in afterwards, got jealous."

"In that case, if he was a married man, his wife could've come in directly afterwards. No need for her to be a lesbian. Her old boyfriend say anything about her being that way?"

"Can't get hold of him. No mention of it yesterday though."

"Where'd you get hold of the idea?"

"Her boss."

"Office gossip."

"Yeah. Probably."

Herbie opens his soft white sandwich, studies its greasy pink inside, closes it. "So what do we know of him?" Herbie lays down the sandwich, makes as if to tick off his fingers, "He's a businessman, and he's married. She met him four years ago. All the businessmen, except one, she was dealing with at that time, live in London, have always lived in the London vicinity. The one outside London, the Preston one, so far as I can make out, has no businesses in London. All his business is up North, or in the Midlands. None of the other three have, or have had, a business address in or near Victoria. None of them live, or have lived, so far as I can find out, in Victoria. None of them appear to go out of London at weekends. And her boyfriend went home only at weekends. Weekdays he was in London."

"Any of these businessmen on the tailors' lists?"

"Not on the three lists we have. And the rest of the tailors are closed."

"This boyfriend definitely went home weekends?"

"According to both Barry Popieluszko and Liz Bradley. And Kate always seemed to be free weekends. Went home to her parents at weekends. Sometimes. Went to visit her brother at weekends. While the boyfriend was with his wife."

Herbie takes up his sandwich, bites into its unresisting softness. It tastes of greasy paper. He chews it into a lump and swallows. Jim has been giving a passable imitation of thought.

"But no one," Herbie says, "knows who he was. Or where she met him. It wasn't through work. It wasn't through her old boyfriend's Camden crowd. A complete stranger. And still a stranger four years on. To us. But to her a murdering bastard who knew her well. Who trusted her to keep stum. Who knew we'd have a job tracing him."

"Know what I read in this police manual once?" Jim says. "Psychology of the criminal, sort of thing. It's always stuck."

"What?"

"The man who believes himself invincible is by that belief made vulnerable."

"That might be of some help if we had some idea who he was."

Herbie again lays down his sandwich, again holds his fingers ready to be ticked off. "Back to basics – motive?"

"Like you said, lovers' tiff." Jim breaks the seal on the whisky bottle, pours into two plastic beakers. "You know how it is – some snotty little reason. Like hardboiling his eggs for the millionth time."

"Not Kate Soames."

"OK then – she was unbearably perfect."

"Possibly."

"Maybe she'd given him the elbow."

"In that case he'd have been there crying over the corpse. All snot, tears and remorse."

Herbie thinks of Mike, takes another bite of his sandwich. "No," he says, "it was an established affair. Four years' standing. Nothing passionate. Just getting on with it. So why suddenly does he kill her?"

"Maybe she was going to blow the whistle on him. Tell his wife. Phone was in her hand."

"Could be. Thanks."

Herbie takes the beaker from Jim, places it beside the remaining half of his sandwich. Jim returns to his desk, puts his feet up. Both find themselves looking at the broken phone on the other desk, meet eyes, grunt.

Herbie finishes the sandwich, frisbees the packaging towards a wastepaper bin. "Yeah. Could be. It's the one thing I don't get about her – that she should put up with him being married. She wasn't the type. Why did she put up with him going home to his wife at weekends? Her old boyfriend, Barry Popieluszko, said that she devotes herself entirely to her man. I just can't see her accepting half shares in return."

"You're sure he was married?"

"That's what Kate told him. And that's the impression Liz Bradley got."

"Liz Bradley?"

"Girl she worked with, used to go on holiday with her."

"Yes. Of course." Jim sips at his whisky. "A businessman … Maybe he'd married the boss's daughter, couldn't risk a divorce."

Herbie purses his lips, shakes his head. "That would've been a weakness. I can't see her tolerating that. Not for four years. Remember – she devoted herself to her man. To his career."

"What if he was married to a cripple or something. Didn't want her hurt. Or he had children?"

"Could be." Herbie rubs his fingers over his lips. "No. Not for four years. She was a hard woman. Has to be another reason."

They sit in silence.

"You not going to drink that?" Jim asks.

"Sorry." Herbie picks up the beaker, "Cheers."

"Maybe she'd just told him he was a lousy screw."

"No," Herbie says. "And why Monday?"

"Has a row with his wife over the weekend. Monday has a row with his girlfriend. Takes it out on her."

"Then why not leave it till the evening? Why phone her at work in the middle of the day? What made him call her up then? It wasn't normal, was enough out of the ordinary to be remarked upon. Something drastic had already happened. What?"

"Like I said – ultimatum from the wife."

"But he had sex with her beforehand. And if the wife's handing out ultimatums, it means that she, the wife, must have already known. So why kill Kate when she's trying to phone her?"

"Maybe she wasn't phoning her."

"Who else?"

They sit in silence again.

"In that case," Jim says, "we're back where we started. Some snotty little reason. Remember that one we had in Wood Green? She killed him because he'd used up all the hot water for his bath. Just got out of hand."

"You're wrong." Herbie beams at him. "This is a big reason. None bigger." He yells a laugh. "This is the end of the world."

"No one knew about it until that night."

"She did, could've convinced him."

"But he phoned her. Phone message got passed on to Bethnal Green. Remember?"

"Damn!" Herbie throws himself back in his chair.

They are silent, until Herbie sits forward, irritably drums his fingers on the desk top, "You're right," he says. "But it still fits. Feels like it fits. Liz Bradley knew all about the end of the world months before it got into the papers. Yet still she went to work on Monday. Then Tuesday, soon as it's been made official, she stops going. Monday morning Kate went to work. Lunchtime she gets a call … and straightaway she stops work. There's got to be a connection."

"OK, but what?"

"All along I've had the feeling that the timing's been important. Just why I don't know. No, it's not timing, it's sequence. That's what's been bugging me. For me the murder came first, then came the news about the end of the world. But the motive fits the end of the world. That's it Jim. We've been looking at it arse about face."

"Even the media though didn't know about it until eight. News came first from America at eight, they said. They took an hour deciding to broadcast it. Put it on the nine o'clock news. Matey phoned her at one, killed her at 4:10."

"Fair enough." Herbie pushes aside the beaker. "But you tell me what else had changed. Everyone's been saying this – he could've saved himself the trouble if he'd known. What if he had known? Up to now we've been looking so hard for the man we've overlooked the motive. Now, maybe, the motive can lead us to the man."

"How could he have known?"

"Just supposing … Look at the effect it's had on everyone else. Suddenly, like this lot who aren't here, they're not in hock to the future anymore. It's got no control over them. No more consequences. Suddenly anything goes. We don't have to care what happens to us any more. No future equals anarchy. Julie goes off to Naples. I row with Sal. He kills Kate."

"A small difference of degree."

"Tomorrow we all die, we're told. So husbands leave wives. Wives leave husbands. Everybody starts going off in different directions. This belongs to the end of the world. It's cars turned over in the street. It's your lot sitting around naked. It's cities on fire. It fits."

"Surely, though, then he'd have killed his wife, got rid of his ball and chain, not his good-time girlfriend?"

"Not necessarily. He's got two women. Suddenly he's forced to make a choice. Kate forces him to make that choice. He kills her. Motive. We've got the motive."

Herbie is excited. Jim is not convinced.

"Now tell me how he knew seven hours ahead of everybody else."

"She was a scientist. Maybe he was an astronomer. Some scientist she met at a convention or something."

"Then why'd she put up with him not leaving his wife?"

"Could've been a civil servant. Boscombe Down. Aldermaston. Somesuch. Didn't want to be seen as a security risk."

"If he was having a bit on the side for four years he was already a security risk. Won't wear, Herbie."

"OK then, like you said, maybe his wife was a cripple. A nervous wreck."

"And I suppose he battered to death our Katherine Helen Soames as a mercy killing? Maybe he was clairvoyant. No," Jim says, "you can't have it all ways."

"Then how did he know?"

"Politician, maybe. That would fit with him not getting a divorce. Bad for his career."

"She didn't like politicians," Herbie says.

He edges the beaker towards him, takes a sip of whisky, places the beaker at arm's length.

"How'd you know she didn't like politicians?" Jim asks.

"Something she wrote," Herbie says. "Something about politicians being liars." Herbie's fingers tap. He stops, looks sharply to Jim. "But that was years ago. Camden days. Living with a radical writer. You're right, Jim." He shakes his finger at him, "You're absolutely bloody right. Hit the nail on the bloody head. Of course you are. Everything fits. It all bloody fits!" Herbie bangs himself on the head. "Been staring me in the face all week. Who goes home every weekend to their wives and constituents?"

"Politicians," Jim supplies the answer.

"And who have long summer holidays?" Herbie holds out his hand for the answer.

"Politicians."

"And who does divorce matter to now? Not you, nor I. Nor most ordinary businessmen. Only the fat cat politicians with their public image. And she wouldn't have wanted to damage his career. Not our Kate. Just think of the scandal. And why, out of all London, did she come to Victoria? She could've got a bigger cheaper flat almost anywhere else. Her work is in Chiswick. Her friends, what friends she had when she moved, all lived in Camden."

"That include the college friend?"

"If she was close, lived close, we'd have turned her up by now. No, our Kate got a flat in Victoria because it's only a matter of minutes from Westminster. Walking distance. And why keep it secret from her friends? Friends she went on holiday with? Because he's in the public eye. Because he's known. And no friend, no matter how close, is going to be able to keep a titbit of juicy gossip like that to herself. And who in the public eye dresses like a businessman? A politician. And who knew about the end of the world before the media? Politicians. We got him, Jim."

"We've narrowed it down to six hundred plus."

"Wrong. We're down to twenty, thirty at the most."

"How'd you make that out?"

"Because we're after a cabinet minister. Or a leader of the opposition. That Minister of the Environment – who was on telly the other night – he said they were told at Monday's Cabinet meeting. Cabinet meetings are held in the mornings. That's when matey knew it was official. And he phoned her at one."

"Just hold your horses, Herbie. If he was a Minister then Mrs Harris would've been bound to have recognised him. She'd have seen him on the telly, in the papers. And even if she hadn't recognised him outright she'd have said he looked familiar."

"Not necessarily. Depends which Minister. If he's been in the news lately. You name me, right now, all twenty Ministers. Of every department."

Herbie, grinning, beckons the answer from him.

"Maybe." Jim holds to his doubts. "Even so, where do we go from here?"

"Think Special Branch'll have their prints?"

"Fat bloody chance they'd let us have them, even if they did."

"What about your mate?"

"He's just a heavy, won't have access to that kind of stuff."

"It's an intro."

"Forget it, Herbie."

"All right, then. What about last year? That terrorist hit list? Twenty-four hour bodyguard for the whole Cabinet? For six months. Your mate might've been in on that. Could've heard a whisper. I can't see our Lothario not paying his mistress a visit for six whole months. Specially not as first thing he does, when he hears the world's about to end, is to get her back home for a screw."

Jim's expression shares neither Herbie's conviction nor his enthusiasm. "I don't know, Herbie."

"Can't hurt just dropping by to see your old marine buddy." Herbie winks at him. "End of the world and all that."

"You know what they're like."

"Come on Jim. Look – do it backwards. Tell 'em we've got this murder in Victoria and we don't want to blunder into a diplomatic incident. Diplomats in the block remember. But say we know one of the Ministers has a girlfriend living there. We don't want our suspect using him as a smokescreen. Say it's an old job, just resurfaced. Not recent, about nine months back." Herbie waves that aside. "No, don't mention the murder. Tell them we've got a mob using a flat there as a drug clearing house. Say we want to charge them for a specific night. And we don't want to embarrass the Minister. We got him, Jim."

"Can't be that easy. How can we be certain it's a Minister?"

"Got any other ideas?"

"Just don't count your chickens." Jim reluctantly stands. "It's still one helluva long shot."

"No, Jim." Herbie rubs his hands together. "We got the bastard."

'... the firm conviction – arising out of a belief in the primitive art of magic, common to all men – that I alone could never die.'
Yukio Mishima. Forbidden Colours. Penguin Books.

Friday: 16:43

Herbie sits at his desk and, for something to do, again studies his report so far. Summarised, he doesn't have much of a case. There had to be as many other reasons for murdering Katherine Helen Soames as there were other circumstances, apart from political, where Katherine Helen Soames would not have pushed her lover for a divorce. Though for the life of him Herbie can't think of any.

Finally Jim comes banging through the office doors. His notebook is held triumphantly aloft. "Good news or the bad news?" he shouts from way off.

"Come on." Herbie impatiently beckons the notebook.

"The bad news," Jim arrives at his desk, has a smug grin that says he isn't going to be hurried with his story, "is that my old buddy isn't there. He's got three young kids. The good news is," he taps his notebook, "there was one man there. Just one man. Greeted me like a long lost brother. And he doesn't think the world is going to end."

"Oh?"

"Reckons it's a plot. 'Don't see our Islamic brethren going barmy over this do you?' An office wallah. Full of statistics. I strung him along, said that I didn't think it was going to happen either, spun him our tale about the drugs."

"And?"

"And he was only too pleased to be of assistance. Said he was sick of picking up the phone and saying sorry, there was nothing he could do. So off we went to look for the relevant files. Wasn't strictly his department, so it took some time."

"That," Herbie taps his watch, "I know."

"But we've got it."

Herbie sits back beaming.

"The bodyguards waited in the basement carpark in," Jim opens his notebook, "August, September and November last year. One Government Minister spent several nights in those flats. Want the dates?"

"That, James, is not what is important."

"Do I hear any guesses to which Government Minister it is who stayed in those flats?"

"Let it be," Herbie holds his hands together in earnest prayer, "the Minister of the Environment."

"Sorry."

"The Arts?"

"Nope."

"Science?"

"Sorry."

"Education?"

"Why education?"

"Paperback beside her bed."

"Give up?" Jim says. Herbie nods. "It was our Minister of Transport."

"Who is?"

"One Michael James Holt. And there's more. Guess where our Minister of Transport's constituency is?"

Herbie spreads his hands.

"Southampton."

"Got him!"

Herbie sits forward and slaps both palms on his desk. "Hook line and bloody sinker." Herbie gets up. "Got him, Jim. Got him. Got him. Got him." Herbie comes exultantly around the desk.

"It's still," Jim raises a cautionary hand, "only a connection."

"No it's not. It's not. When she was ditching her Polish boyfriend," Herbie affectionately pats the photograph of Barry Popieluszko, "when she was dumping our untidy friend here, she was going down to her brother's practically every weekend. In Southampton. Which is Michael James Holt's constituency. It fits, Jim."

"But think, Herbie, would you charge him on this alone? In normal circumstances?"

"In normal circumstances Mike would already have been ringing the panic bells in the corridors of power."

"I still don't get the motive," Jim says. "He kills her because she's going to cause a scandal? They both knew the world was going to end in six days, so what's it matter who she tells? What would a scandal matter?"

"Like you said, these aren't normal circumstances."

"We got any corroborating evidence then?" Jim says. "He on any of the tailors' lists?"

"No." Herbie again checks each. "No. But our conscientious colleague only got three done prior to bunking off for the duration."

"What about the blood group, then? Being a politician he's bound to have been a donor. Good public relations."

"Hospitals are all closed."

"Don't matter. I can tie in with their records from here. Won't take a minute."

Jim moves to a keyboard.

"Still be only circumstantial," Herbie tells him. Jim is running a finger down the columns of a booklet. "Be one more brick,

Herbie." He finds the code, begins typing. Herbie walks twice around the office.

"I'm popping up to Mike's office. Get his *Who's Who*."

Herbie runs up the stairs, charges into Mike's office. That it has been trashed doesn't surprise Herbie. Phones have been thrown against the wall, picture frames smashed, drawers pulled out and stamped through, shelves swiped clean, files ripped in half.

Careful of glass shards, Herbie pushes aside debris, finds the book. Flipping its pages to rid it of dust and glass splinters he starts leafing through it as he walks back along the corridor. Coming down the stairs he pauses. He smiles, nods and smiles, and continues on down the stairs.

Jim is still at the keyboard.

"Found him," Herbie says. "Oxford educated. And his declared interests are two directorships. One in a computer company, one in an electronics firm. Recreation – musical soirées. Got to be him." He slaps the heavy book closed and dumps it onto a desk.

"Hold on a minute," Jim says.

"Reckon that Fleet Street shop will still be open?" Herbie asks him.

"Don't see why not." Jim is watching the screen, clicking the mouse, waiting for new icons, clicking the mouse.

"Did they have any milk?"

"Can't remember." Jim taps in some numbers.

"What we'll do is this," Herbie says. "We'll get some mug shots from here. Forty, fifty-year-old businessmen. And someone's still writing newspapers, so we'll call into one of the press offices, wangle a photo of our Minister out of them. And a couple of not so obvious Ministers. Then we'll get some milk from that shop and deliver it to Mrs Harris. Got it?"

The screen is scrolling down a list of names.

"Got it," Jim says, grin growing. "Michael James Holt, Southampton address, blood group O positive."

"Satisfied now?" Herbie asks him.

"Nearly there."

"Let's go then." Herbie is half way to the door.

"Just think," Jim says as he catches up with him in the corridor, "if he hadn't left that door open."

"Like you said," Herbie claps him on the shoulder, "the invincible man's one oversight."

'Who will write the obituary of the man who outlives all his friends?'
Barry Popieluszko. Happy Robot Goes Cosmic: Fire Dragon.

'Years sneaked past, an unseen metamorphosis, young into old ...'
Barry Popieluszko. Raw As Birth: White Swan.

Friday: 18:36

The dog snuffles at, yaps at, the door.

"Brought you some milk, Mrs Harris." Herbie holds the carton of UHT milk up to the spyhole. Mrs Harris is already undoing the locks.

"You shouldn't have bothered." She opens the door. "Old lady like me." She beckons them gladly into the flat.

Herbie and Jim wait while she closes the door. The little dog runs yelping around their feet. Mrs Harris, fussing and chiding the dog, telling it about the milk, goes before them into the living room.

"We do want something in return," Herbie says when she's quieted the dog.

"What's that?"

"Some photographs for you to look at. See if our friend from next door is among them."

"Would you like a cup of tea? Now I've got some milk."

"No thanks. We're running a bit late as it is."

Mrs Harris releases the dog and importantly arranges herself in her chair. Jim pulls a low table before her, and picks up the dog, which is circling his legs.

Herbie removes the photographs from their large brown envelopes, hands the first to Mrs Harris.

"Just a minute." She regally holds up her hand. "Pass me my glasses please. Over there."

Jim fetches them from the sideboard.

"Now, take your time," Herbie tells her.

Mrs Harris scrutinises the first photograph, hands it back to Herbie, who returns it to the bottom of the pile and gives her the next photograph.

While she examines that photograph Jim draws Herbie's attention to the open kitchen door. The draining board has dirty glasses on it. The rubbish bin too is full. In a bowl of fruit on the sideboard is a rotten apple, white-spotted brown.

The photograph of Michael James Holt, silver grey hair, black eyebrows, is the fifth that Mrs Harris looks at.

"That's him," she says. Jim and Herbie remain professionally impassive. The dog tries to lick Jim's face.

"Keep going," Herbie tells Mrs Harris. "Don't want to make a mistake."

Mrs Harris hesitates over the two photographs of the lesser-known Cabinet Ministers, comes to the last photograph.

Herbie pats them all together, places the stack on the table. "Can you go back through them, please, Mrs Harris, pick out the one you recognised. At this stage we can't afford to go off on a wild goose chase."

She again carefully examines each photograph before handing it back to Herbie. And she stops again at the photograph of Michael James Holt.

"Hundred percent certain," she says. "This is him." She prods the photograph. "Who is he?"

"His name is Michael James Holt. Most people know him as our Minister of Transport."

"D'you know," she takes off her glasses, "I thought I recognised him the first time I saw him. Well, listen, Inspector," she passes the rest of the photographs over to Herbie, "don't you let his being a Minister stop you. What he did to that poor girl was terrible. And to think a man like that's a Minister of the Crown. You get him, Inspector."

"Don't worry, Mrs Harris." Jim places the panting dog in her lap. "Inspector Watkins is not the type to let a little thing like that stand in his way."

"Well," she gleefully cuddles the dog, "if the end of the world can't stop him, I don't suppose anything can."

"Thank you for all your help, Mrs Harris." Herbie slides the photographs back into the envelope, tucks the envelope under his arm. "Jason too. Without him we'd never have found out in time."

"See. You've been good for something in your worthless life," she tells the dog. "It's been very interesting, Inspector. And thank you for the milk. You go and get him now."

"We will."

Waiting for the lift Jim and Herbie listen to Mrs Harris put the chain across the door to number twenty three, tell her dog about Michael James Holt, Minister of Transport …

"A bloody politician." Jim, shaking his head, enters the lift.

"You can't be that surprised, Jim," Herbie says. "They're all unprincipled bloody hooligans. Look at the promises they make, and break. Every time. You and I don't sell our principles for a few votes. To make ourselves popular. We accept the consequences of our principles, pay the price and keep our self-respect. With them it's all means to an end. They sell their nation's pride for a penny. Look at that Environment Minister. Toe rag."

"We going down to Southampton now?"

"Time we get there and back it'll be gone midnight." They step out of the lift into the underground car park. "No, we'll go back to The Yard, fill up the tank, start off first thing. What you got on tonight?"

"Dunno." They have come to a stop on either side of the car. "Hadn't thought about it." Jim gets into the driving seat.

"Why don't you come over to Walworth," Herbie says as he does up his seatbelt, "sleep the night, leave first thing together?"

"No thanks, Herb." Jim starts the car. "You'll want to be with Sal, on your own, at a time like this."

"Sal'll be pleased to see you." They ride up the ramp into daylight. "And to be honest – we've been playing cards and stuff – it'd be better with three of us. Just the two of you, you get to know each other's game."

Jim has turned left towards Westminster.

"You're just after the most expensive whisky in the world," Jim says.

"We've been working together too long." Herbie makes a found-out face. "You can read my mind."

"Look at it." Jim signifies the few cars in the street ahead. "The rush hour."

'Life reaches no resolutions, just proceeds from one inconclusive muddle to another state of waiting.'

Barry Popieluszko. The Watcher: Kerala Books.

Friday: 22:12

"Watkins."

"Dad?"

"Hello darlin'. Where're you now?"

"Other side of Pisa." Her voice is faint.

"Where?"

"On the other side of Pisa. Took us all morning to get through the border."

The line clicks and burps.

"All morning? How was that? Queues?"

"Queues? No. They've re-instated the border. And you got to go through by road: they got the rest of it mined. I was all for chancing it, but Peter said we'd try another crossing."

"Good for Peter."

"He said if he only had two days left he wanted those two days."

"But you're in Italy now?"

"The other side of Pisa. We went like hell this afternoon to make up for lost time. If we get an early start we should make Naples tomorrow."

"So how did you get through the border?"

"I thought you'd have known."

The line warbles and bleeps.

"Sorry darlin', this is a terrible line. And I'm afraid we been drinking. Jim's here. We been playing cards. Your Mum's mad as hell 'cos she keeps losing. Reckons me and Jim are conspiring against her."

"Give it here." Sal pokes him in the side. He misses what Julie was saying,

"What's that?"

"I said I can hear you all right. Give Jim my love."

"How should I have already known?"

"I told this border guard who my father was. He phoned New Scotland Yard and they let us through."

"Yeah? Told you – long arm of the law. Here's your Mum. Going frantic here. Both of you get there in one piece." Herbie frowns. "If you see what I mean."

Sal takes the phone.

"What?" she says loudly. "Yes, your father's blotto. And I'm not far behind." Sal sniggers. "What's that?"

Herbie resumes his seat opposite Jim, smiles at him. "Julie." He inclines his head towards the phone. "Got past Pisa. You get any calls from Italy today?"

"No." Jim thinks. "No. Why?"

"They wouldn't let 'em through the border. So Julie," Herbie lifts a finger, "she got this border guard to phone the Yard. And they let 'em through."

"Yeah?" Jim smiles. "Wonder who he spoke to?"

"She sends her love to you."

"Julie?"

"Yeah."

They listen to Sal; saying yes into the phone.

"Just think," Jim says. "Detective Inspector Herbie Watkins of International Repute."

The laughter snorts out of them. Sal hushes them.

"What's that, love?" she says into the phone. "Dunno. Right coupla clowns. Oh, have you? All right then, love. I love you too. Take care. Bye. Don't …" Sal takes the phone away from her face. "She's gone."

'... no one screams when you destroy their dreams. (They didn't exist; how, therefore, can they die? How can they be lamented?) After the death of a dream there is deflation only, and depression ...'

Barry Popieluszko. Raw As Birth. White Swan.

Saturday: 09:03

Sal places a large red thermos and a Tupperware box of sandwiches on the kitchen table.

"What's this for?" Herbie looks up to her. "Shouldn't take us that long."

"Might. And you're not likely to find anywhere open today. Besides, state you two're in, some coffee'll do you good."

"Question is," Jim says, "is there enough there? Way my head feels I could drink a gallon. Any more tea in that pot?"

"Sure you don't fancy a trip out in the country, love?" Herbie takes hold of Sal's free hand as she reaches across the table for Jim's cup. "I can't see this Southampton business taking us more than an hour. We could run down to the seaside afterwards."

"I'm sure Jim'd love that."

Sal takes her hand away, refills Jim's cup.

"Wouldn't mind. Thanks." Jim takes the cup, spoons sugar into it. "Used to like being at sea. Might even have a dip. Got any spare trunks, Herb?"

"Go on, love," Herbie turns in his seat, "bit of fresh air do you the power."

Sal picks her rubber gloves off the draining board. "I don't think so." She pulls on the gloves. "Anyway, I've told Mum I'm coming."

"Give her a ring."

"No." Sal begins washing the breakfast dishes. "I'd like to see her. You know …"

"All right, love. We'll wrap it up as quick as we can. Give your Mum my love."

Jim lifts his elbows off the table, yawns. "You ever fancy being a country copper Herbie? Nice quiet life."

"All they get is to chase stray cows."

"Is it?"

"What," Sal asks Herbie, "you going to do if it doesn't end tomorrow?"

"Wait and see."

"What I don't get," Jim says, "is what we're going to do when we get there."

"Play it by ear."

"Just be careful." Sal gathers up dishes from the table. Her gloves drip foamy water onto the Tupperware pack. "Don't want anything to happen to you now." The dishes go into the sink. "And try not to be too long, love." A wet glove grips Herbie's shoulder. "Just in case."

'A state of mind that sees a profound sadness in life's repetitions ... The young following the same old dreams.'

Barry Popieluszko. Psychotic Android Eats: Fire Dragon.

'When young he had wanted to be someone with a past. Now that he was that someone he didn't want his past.'

Barry Popieluszko. Raw As Birth: White Swan.

'Furniture shined and polished in a house. The house destroyed. What meaning the life that shined and polished?'

Barry Popieluszko. The Watcher: Kerala Books.

Saturday: 12:05

The country house is enclosed by woodland, has a long gravel drive, ivy-clad facade, pillared portico.

Jim and Herbie stand on the front doorstep, tall white double doors before them. Somewhere in the rear of the house is the bark of a big dog.

Jim is holding a briefcase.

Footsteps come clacking across a tiled floor within. One of the doors is opened by a woman in her late forties, long grey hair done up loosely, full figure.

"Mrs Holt?" Herbie says. "Detective Inspector Watkins. Detective Sergeant Nixon. New Scotland Yard." Both show her their IDs. "We've come to see your husband."

She smiles, amused by their stern formality, stands aside for them to enter.

Stairs come down the centre of the hall, passages off to either side. Mrs Holt indicates a door deep in the wall on their left. "He's in there. Don't bother knocking. Got his headphones on."

"Do I wait here?" Jim hands Herbie the briefcase. Herbie takes the briefcase, nods.

"One of those meetings, is it?" Mrs Holt cheerily says. "You don't want to hang around here then, Sergeant. Come into the kitchen. I was just about to prepare some lunch. Though I'm sure I can delay that to make us a cup of tea."

Jim looks to Herbie. "I'll holler if I need you," Herbie tells him.

Jim follows the wide-hipped Mrs Holt along the passageway to the left of the stairs.

Herbie quietly opens the deepset door.

A long room, French windows at the far end, beige carpet, some rugs, polished antiques. Library-cum-office. Bookshelves flanking the marble fireplace. Blue-bound Hansards. Above the mantle an oil-painting of a gravy-coloured ancestor. Opposite the fireplace an open scroll-top desk. A low marble-topped table near the windows, beside it a reclining chair, its back to Herbie.

Michael James Holt, headphones on over thick grey hair, is sitting in that chair.

Beyond the French windows is a stone balustrade, then a long lawn leading down to a stand of summer dark trees.

Herbie softly closes the door, slowly approaches the reclining chair. (The reclining chair is a comparatively modern piece at odds with the rest of the tasteful antique furniture in the long room.

Michael James Holt is a man who likes his comforts. At any price?)

The hands of Michael James Holt are resting on the arms of the chair. Large flat thumbs.

In the glass ashtray on the marble-topped table are two long stubs. From the headphones comes the faintly audible warble of an operatic soprano.

Not wanting to appear stealthy, but as quietly as he can, on his raised knee Herbie opens the briefcase, switches on the recorder. He scratches a fingernail across the microphone grill to make sure it is working. With both feet back on the floor Herbie holds the briefcase closed with his hand.

Reaching over the back of the chair Herbie lightly taps Michael James Holt on the shoulder.

Except for the surprise on his face Michael James Holt looks like his photograph – thick black brows, sharp nose, smooth cheeks, silvered hair swept back from the temples. One fat cat. One fat dirty cat – the front of his striped shirt is streaked with fag ash and drink dribbles. (Kate Soames hadn't changed types when she'd left Barry Popieluszko: she had simply, with little else to do, kept her home in order.)

Headphones still on, still warbling, Michael James Holt converts his surprise into a frown at Herbie.

Herbie displays his ID.

With a mouth-pursing grimace Michael James Holt reaches over to the stereo on his other side, switches it off and, careful of his hair, removes the headphones.

"Detective Inspector Watkins," Herbie introduces himself, sets the briefcase down on the low table.

"I thought," Michael Holt sits, feet now on the floor, half-turned towards Herbie, "we'd cleared everything away yesterday."

Michael James Holt hasn't shaved for at least the last two days. Hasn't cleaned his teeth either: the breath of sleep blasting

Herbie's way. Neat and clean herself, what was it Kate Soames liked about dirty men? The excitement of the unclean?

"I know nothing about yesterday," Herbie says quietly.

"Christ," Michael Holt says, "you bloody people …"

"I'm from New Scotland Yard," Herbie interrupts him. "I am investigating the murder of one Katherine Helen Soames."

Michael Holt's eyes have dodged to the floor, to the window, back to Herbie. "And just what the hell's that got to do with me, Inspector?"

"Michael James Holt," Herbie says, "I feel that I should warn you now that this interview is being recorded." Herbie indicates the briefcase.

Politicians are used to bluffing. "I repeat, Inspector, what the hell's that got to do with me?"

"Michael James Holt, I have reason to believe that last Monday, at ten past four in the afternoon, you battered to death one Katherine Helen Soames."

"Get out of here!" Michael Holt makes a show of getting to his feet, made awkward by the footrest of the reclining chair being raised, ends up sitting awkwardly upright. "I've got better things to do, on my last afternoon on Earth, than listen to this rubbish."

Michael James Holt is a man used to wielding power, to being obeyed.

Herbie is used to people protesting their innocence, hasn't moved, hasn't batted even an eyelid.

"We can conduct this interview here, Sir," Herbie says, "or at the local police station. Whichever you prefer."

"Just who d'you think you're kidding? For a start," MP Michael James Holt gestures broadly, "I doubt there's a police station still open in the whole of Southampton."

The outflung hand is trembling.

"In that case, Sir, I'll have to take you back to London with me."

"And what if I refuse to accompany you? If I should resist?"

"I'd overcome that resistance, Sir."

Michael James Holt is not as tall as Herbie.

"You think so?" he asks craftily.

"My Sergeant is outside the door."

Michael Holt looks from the door to the French windows.

"And if you think you can run away, Sir, my Sergeant and I will pursue you." Michael Holt lowers his silver-haired head. The hair is greasy. "Are we to conduct this interview here, Sir, or in London?"

Michael James Holt slightly raises his head. Although bowed, the pose is one of furious concentration, not contrition. Reaching a decision, Michael James Holt slowly lies back.

Herbie takes the hard chair from before the desk, positions himself opposite Michael Holt, the low table at an angle between them, briefcase open upon it.

"Where were you between the hours of two and six last Monday afternoon?" Herbie asks him.

"Is this absolutely necessary?"

"Yes."

"But why, man? Why? The world is about to end any minute: what on earth do you hope to gain from this persecution?"

Heating up, the man smells of acidic two-day sweat.

"Persecution, Sir? I have reason to believe that you brutally murdered Katherine Helen Soames."

"Is this some personal vendetta? Because of my position? Because I am a Cabinet Minister?"

"So far as I am concerned you are simply a member of the public whom I believe to have committed a crime."

"Bullshit. You're telling me that if your suspect had turned out to be some South London villain you'd be wasting your last afternoon on him?"

"I did not discover your identity until late yesterday afternoon. If, as you say, I'd had reason to suspect a South London villain of this crime, then I'd have been visiting him today."

"But why, man? Why? No matter what evidence you think you've got this'll never come to court. The world, unless you've been so busy you haven't heard, ends some time today."

"Maybe that's all the more reason."

"One of my Cabinet colleagues, Inspector, committed suicide. Because the world was about to end. Tell me where's the logic in that? Where's the logic in what you're doing?" He gives Herbie no time to answer. "You drive down here today? There's bodies left rotting in those wrecks."

"I don't see the connection."

"There's riots, looting, pillage dammit everywhere. Why bother with this one murder?"

"Because this is the case to which I was assigned. Now, if you don't mind, Sir, if we could –"

"Who's your superior officer?"

"There's no one there, Sir."

"Then what the hell do you want from me?"

"The truth."

"How do I know you are who you say you are? That ID could be stolen. What is this, some shakedown?"

"Shall I call my Sergeant?"

"How much do you want?" Michael Holt again makes as if to stand.

"You're being ridiculous, Sir."

"Then what d'you want?"

"The truth."

"And that's all? Just the truth?"

"For today, yes."

"Fuck off out of here." Michael Holt dismisses him.

Herbie was expecting such defiance. The man is a bully: Herbie, though, is physically bigger than him. Herbie looks at the face in profile: was Kate attracted to this plummy twat because he reminded her of her father? Seeking the affection that that pompous old git had decided the child didn't need?

Enough of all this highfalutin' crap, Herbie tells himself, back to basics.

Levering himself forward Herbie grabs Michael James Holt's shirt collar, twists it in his fist and pushes it hard – with all his body weight – down into the angle of Michael Holt's neck. Michael James Holt is pinned into the reclining chair staring straight into Herbie's other large fist.

"Listen, you big fat smelly bastard," Herbie says in almost a whisper, "you start giving me the runaround and I'll fuckin' pulverise you." The chair springs creak. Michael Holt's mouth works in fear. "My Sergeant won't hear a thing. And we're anyway of a like mind, him and I. So no more shit! Understand me?"

White spittle has formed in the corners of Michael Holt's mouth. The hair gives off a musky reek.

"Understand me?"

Michael Holt nods once.

Herbie releases him, slowly sits back on the hard chair. Michael Holt rotates his neck.

"Should I," he looks meekly at Herbie, "just supposing, confess to this preposterous charge, what then? Back to London?"

"No, Sir," Herbie says in his usual tone, "I don't believe we any longer have facilities for prisoners. No, if you should confess, and if the world has not ended on Monday, then I'll be back for you on Monday."

"And if I deny anything to do with this murder?"

"It's a simple matter of taking your prints and checking them against the prints found on the murder weapon. You can voluntarily give me your prints here, now; or I can formally charge you, take you back to London, and take your prints there."

"Thought you said there were no facilities for prisoners?" he cleverly asks, despite his fear.

"There aren't. But, should you prove obstructive, there's nothing to stop me locking you up myself."

"Got no bloody choice, have I? You bastard. This is blackmail."

Michael Holt's pomposity and defiance are at odds with his ungroomed appearance, with the uncertainty and fear in his eyes.

"Matters are complicated at the moment, are slightly irregular," Herbie plays the game, "In normal circumstances, given the evidence I've got, I would already have charged you, and you would now be in police custody."

"In normal circumstances, with such an outrageous charge, and with such intimidating behaviour, believe me, Inspector, you would never have got this close."

"I prefer to believe I would, Sir. So if you wouldn't mind giving me your fingerprints and answering some questions?" Herbie puts out his hand to the briefcase.

Michael Holt holds up both hands, a gesture as much a plea as intended to halt Herbie. "You do realise," his voice now quietly reasonable, putting himself on Herbie's side, "that if this does come to court this interview will be construed as having been conducted under duress?" The eyes ask not to be hit, try to reconcile this Herbie, all politeness, with the one who had had him by the shirt.

"In court all things are possible, Sir," Herbie says. "I feel it's fair to warn you, however, that we do have other evidence."

"Such as?"

"Such as what I believe to be your prints, your blood group, your genetic coding, your suit material ..."

"Circumstantial."

186

"You were seen leaving the flat."

"Who by?"

"That I'm not prepared to divulge, Sir. Now could I take your prints?"

In silence Herbie takes the ink pad and sheet of card from the briefcase, arranges them on the table.

Michael Holt is studying the revolving cassette wheels. "Can we turn that off?"

"Afraid not, Sir."

"Let me get this straight," Michael Holt says. "No matter what I say today, if I admit to ten murders and high treason, you're not going to do anything about it until Monday?"

"I am simply collecting evidence today."

"And if I should tell you what you've come here to hear, you're not going to do anything about it until Monday?"

"All I'm after today is the truth."

"All right then, let me put it this way – if I should confess, then you'll leave me here the rest of this weekend?"

"Whatever you choose to tell me now will not be acted upon until Monday. I'll take your prints now – one way or another – and should they match the prints found on the murder weapon, then that will be damning evidence enough."

"So if I confess now I'll be left here until Monday?"

"Yes."

"So, if the world ends this afternoon, only you and I will know what was said here?"

"And my Sergeant."

"No one else?"

"Not until Monday. Now if I could take your prints?"

Michael Holt hesitates. Still not sure which side of Herbie to believe – the professional or the thug. Then, with a smile to humour the madman, he gives up his left hand to Herbie.

Herbie proceeds to ink and press each finger. Handing him a tissue from the briefcase, Herbie then fingerprints the right hand.

While Michael Holt is wiping his fingers and thumbs Herbie signs and dates the sheet of card, returns it to the briefcase.

Michael Holt has lit a cigarette. All Kate's close friends smoked. Kate didn't. Liz Bradley had had a holiday affair. Kate hadn't. Miss Self-Righteous? Sought out naughty people because she didn't dare be naughty herself? Still no reason for her to get killed.

"Is that your red Rover in the garage?" Herbie asks Michael Holt.

"It is."

"Did you drive that car to Katherine Helen Soames's block of flats on Monday?"

"What do you hope to gain from this?" Michael Holt studies Herbie. "You yourself? A place in heaven?"

"Peace of mind," Herbie says. "Was that red Rover the car you drove to Katherine Helen Soames's block of flats on Monday?"

Michael James Holt makes a decision. "It was."

"You had sex with her?"

"I did."

"And then you killed her?"

"No." It is said fiercely.

Herbie gives Michael James Holt, red in the face, a long sideways look. "I think we'd better go back to London." He reaches for the briefcase. "Check the prints and then talk."

"All right. All right. Hold your horses. What I was trying to say was that I never meant to kill her, dammit."

"Why did you hit her?"

"Because she was trying to phone my wife."

"And tell her of your liaison?"

"I'm not going to have it come out this way."

With a sharp jab Michael Holt stubs out the partly smoked cigarette. "Sounds so bloody sordid. No. If this is going to be told, Inspector, it's going to be told my way."

"As you wish."

Michael James Holt takes a deep breath, looks about the room, and plunges. "Kate and I have been seeing each other for three years or more. She took care of my needs in town, you might say. And it's no great shakes a Minister having a mistress, you know: Lloyd-George had several. And Kate was discreet. Quiet. More like a wife than my wife, if you know what I mean." He has glanced to the door, lowered his voice. "And I suppose, if it hadn't been for this end of the world thing, we'd have gone on quietly for years."

Herbie waits for him to continue, has to prompt him, "What difference did the end of the world make? Apart from the obvious?"

"Kate had been on about it for months. I partly believed her: but it all seemed so academic. Years and years away. Then suddenly, last Monday morning, I'm told by the Prime Minister that we've all got six days left. My own world ended there and then."

"So you phoned Kate?" Herbie again has to prompt him.

"Soon as I could get away. Told her it was official. You see, she was the only one I could talk to about it. She already knew. And I was literally stunned. I'm still not sure that I truly believe it. But I do; wouldn't be telling you this now if I didn't."

He has tried to sound brave to himself. Doesn't. "That was the state of mind I was in when I met her in the flat. And, like you said, we had sex. More out of habit than for pleasure. What else was there to do? Then afterwards … afterwards Kate started going on about how there was no reason now for keeping up the charade. What did it matter, now, who knew? She didn't give me time to think. I've always led her to believe that mine hasn't been a happy marriage. Nor has it been at times. It has, though, its compensations. Kate's logic, not giving an inch, was impeccable. She wouldn't give me chance to explain. To think, even. We can stay here, she was saying. No need to go home, we can get whatever you need here. An end to all that, she said. Let's finish honestly."

He pauses, thinking back over the scene. Herbie gives him time.

"I suppose I must have appeared less than keen on the idea. I made a few practical objections; but Kate easily over-rode them, just went on making plans for me regardless. She guessed, though, the way I was thinking. So, when I said that I felt I ought to at least go home and explain to my wife, she dug her heels in, asked what was wrong with the phone. Held out the phone to me."

Michael James Holt sighs. "I'd told Kate that my wife and I have led separate existences for years. Which is true. She's got her horses and her children: I've got Parliament and my constituents. Though it's not anywhere near as clear-cut as that. Not that I could explain that to Kate. And Kate, seeing that I wasn't going to phone my wife, she decided to take matters into her own hands."

Some men cry when they confess, some stutter; Michael James Holt, though, is used to having secrets, is used to disclosing them, to selecting his words with care. He is, however, sweating. And the hotter he gets the more the old sweat in his clothes heats up. Herbie moves back a nostril's pace.

"She phoned?" Herbie says.

"Tried to. I was shouting at her things like Let's not be rash. Don't be stupid. And every time she dialled I cut her off. I was walking and shouting at her. Don't be ridiculous. But every time I cut her off she just began dialling again. Next thing I know I had some ornament in my hand."

"You hit her?"

"No. Yes I did. I didn't mean to. I don't think I meant to. I tried to smash the phone. But, somehow, I hit her arm. She didn't cry out or anything. Just looked at me. Shock, I suppose. I can see that now. But that's when I completely lost my temper and hit her on the head."

"How many times did you hit her on the head?"

"I don't know. Until her eyes shut."

"And then what?"

"Then ... then I realised what I'd done, tried to pull myself together. Then I saw that if I could get away with it for a week, just a week, I was safe. Or as safe as any of us would be. So I began clearing out anything that might implicate me. Obviously I didn't succeed."

"At what time did you leave the flat?"

"Must've been gone five."

"You stayed in the flat for over an hour after you attacked her? You did check that she was dead?"

"Wasn't she? Is that ... No, she was. No doubt about it. And I couldn't have phoned an ambulance anyway – the phone was broken. You've got to realise my world had just collapsed. If this does come to court I'll probably plead diminished responsibility. Temporary insanity. I'm not sure of the exact procedures, but I suspect," he dares to say, "that this interview is highly irregular. So this, as testimony, is probably invalid. Not that I'm trying to escape the consequences of what I did. But, you've got to admit, they were such strange circumstances."

"You were about to get found out."

"No. No way. My whole life had just ended. All that I'd striven for. Christ – I'm an *almost* man. I've been an MP for thirteen years now. This was my first full Ministerial position. The future was mine, dammit. Last Monday morning it was stolen from me."

He dwells on the injustice of that. Herbie moves to ask a question. Michael James Holt, however, now wants to explain every nut and bolt nuance of the whole affair. "Do you know what it's like waiting to be noticed? For years I've felt my potential's been unused, that I've been living in the shadow of my own existence, my true reserves unknown and untapped." He's quoting, Herbie knows. This is just conversation now. "I was skimming along on life's edges," he says. "And there, at last! I was in the centre of things. Only for it to be stolen from me last Monday morning. Stolen! I sat in that Cabinet room in silence, let the others speak their piece. What did it matter?"

"Did you give Kate a watch?"

Michael James Holt frowns irritably at Herbie's interruption, contains his anger, remembers his fear. "Yes."

"And you took it from the flat after you killed her?"

"Yes."

"And her diary?"

"Yes."

"Where are they?"

"Wristwatch I threw out of the car window on the M3. All the paper I burnt here. Bonfire."

"How did you originally meet Kate?"

"Her brother is one of my constituents. Had a nervous breakdown, was dismissed from his job. I can't recall the exact details. He was said not to be eligible for any benefits. Kate came to me to sort it out for him."

"In Southampton?"

"At first. London later. I'd expected some left-wing harridan, got Kate. I took her to lunch a couple of times. Then we started shacking up in hotels. Then she got the flat in Victoria."

"Why didn't you lock the flat door when you left Monday?"

"I'd put the latch up – to get my case out. Then I heard the lift coming. I didn't want to be seen near the flat, so I dodged down the stairs."

"Your wife didn't know about Kate?"

"Not a thing. No reason why she should. Kate understood how damaging a divorce would be. If anything she was the sensible one. I offered her a better job once in one of my companies. She turned it down, said that it'd be too obvious. She believed in me, in all that I hoped to achieve."

"You're Transport. Why was Kate reading a book on education?"

"Was a reshuffle mooted. Whisper was that Education was mine. Look, this must make me sound a right rotten bastard. It wasn't like that though. I didn't set out to use her; it just happened that way. Of course I saw myself as a bit of a lad having a mistress in London. But it was all very domestic. You see, when it came down to it, Kate was more of a wife than my wife. With Kate, of necessity, I was very much a stay-at-home. My wife likes parties. Nor is it just that. You see, like any man I suppose, I occasionally resent my family, the demands they make on me. What they expect as their right of me. Kate though made no demands, expected nothing of me. All I had to do with her was relax, make love to her. Do you know how much that ensnares you? Come the end I felt more beholden to her than I did to my wife and children. Because she expected nothing of me. Until Monday."

"Then you refused to pay?"

"It wasn't that. Not that at all." He is prepared to defy Herbie with the truth. "I felt that I'd acquitted myself to my family. Could meet them as equals. With them I knew exactly where I stood. I knew what they wanted of me, what I had given them. But Kate ... Kate I just owed. You're right, I didn't know how I could pay her off. Kate I owed too much; and the only way I could pay her off was by staying with her. And that I didn't want to do. Because, forced to make a choice, I realised that where I wanted to be was at home with my wife. Because, when it came down to it, it was my wife who was the reality. It was Kate who was the charade."

"So you killed her?"

"Yes."

They are silent. Herbie consults his notebook.

"Thank you, Mr Holt." He closes it. "Is there anything else you wish to tell me?"

"That's it?"

"Yes."

"You're going now?"

"I'll be back Monday." Herbie reaches towards the briefcase. "If we're all still here."

He shuts off the recorder, closes the case.

"You're leaving now?"

"Yes." Herbie stands, picks up the briefcase.

"Thank you, Inspector," Michael James Holt scrambles off the reclining chair to hold out his hand, "for being so understanding. For giving me my freedom this afternoon."

Herbie ignores the hand. "I'll be back Monday."

"And I'll be here, Inspector. If we are, that is."

Michael James Holt is smiling now, a burden gone from him. He is pleased to have confessed, had wanted someone to confide in, can now meet the end of the world with a settled conscience.

Herbie starts walking towards the door. "I wasn't being strictly honest when I said," Herbie stops with his hand on the doorknob, "that only you, my Sergeant and I would know what was said in here. While I have been interviewing you my Sergeant has been interviewing your wife."

"My wife?"

The smile sticks to Michael James Holt's face. His hand reaches out to the back of the reclining chair.

"He's been asking her where you were on Monday afternoon, what she knows of Katherine Helen Soames, did she know of your affair with her. Your wife won't know precisely what was said in here; no doubt though she'll draw her own conclusions."

Herbie turns the doorknob, pauses to study Michael James Holt. "The end of the world, even the end of the world, can't excuse what you did to that girl. It was a brutal cowardly murder." Herbie opens the door. "I'm sorry for your wife. I couldn't, though, let you get away with it."

'Never forget the guilt of the victim. Did they/didn't they deserve what happened to them? Did they/didn't they collude?'

Barry Popieluszko. Happy Robot Goes Cosmic: Fire Dragon.

'Like the young – always – we too had our future betrayed... Forgetfulness of routine eases the pain; until we see the young again being betrayed ...'

Barry Popieluszko. Psychotic Android Eats: Fire Dragon.

Saturday: 13:52

Herbie sits with the briefcase on his lap.

Jim drives, waits for Herbie to tell him what happened. Herbie has not spoken since he summoned Jim from the kitchen and they left the house.

A black car overtakes them.

"What did you make of the wife?" Herbie asks.

"All right. Bit county. Gave me a load of milk." On the back seat is a shallow cardboard box packed tightly with different sized jamjars.

"They keep cows?"

"No. She said she rode over to a local farm early this morning. Apparently the tankers aren't picking up the milk. Farmers are just tipping it. 'Cos even if they take the milk themselves to the bottling factories, the factories aren't fully automatic, so it just gets tipped down the drain there. And they can't stop milking the cows. Hurts 'em if they're not milked. Milk fever. A couple of the local farmers have had their whole herds put down, she said."

"They believe it, then?"

"The stars, Herbie. They can see 'em here."

Jim slows past a wreck. "Was it him?"

"Yeah." Herbie pats the briefcase. "Like you said, she blew the whistle on him. And he wanted his home comforts. To slob out his last days."

"Bastard." Jim accelerates.

"Yeah. Smelly bastard. Deceived two women, ended up killing one of 'em. That's about the sum of it."

"Like crosswords," Jim says, "always seems so bloody simple once you know the answers."

"The wife have any inkling why we were there?"

"No. They had people down there yesterday collecting papers. MI5 or somebody."

"I told him you were asking her about Katherine Helen Soames."

Jim glances to Herbie, back to the road ahead. He chuckles. "Neat. Very neat. He's going to blow the whistle on himself. Yeah, neat. Hoisted by his own petard. If he asks her he tells her. And if he doesn't ask her he thinks she's only acting normal for the sake of it. In fact there's no way he can find out if she really does or doesn't know without telling her. Yeah. Neat, Herbie."

"Why do I always feel so bloody let down, though? Even when they get put away. Never seems enough somehow. Solves nothing. Proves nothing. All that trouble we go to. Suddenly it's over."

"Name of the game."

Jim drives.

"His children there?" Herbie asks.

"Sound like a right bunch of Hoorays. Been in London for an End of the World Ball. She's off to a Last Tango In Southampton tonight. Was wondering what to wear."

"What you doing tonight?"

"Dunno."

"Sal's cooking up a cordon bleu blow-out. You're welcome."

"All the same to you, Herbie, I fancy going off somewhere on my own, getting quietly tanked. See if I can find some other lost and lonely soul to screw away the night."

"Fair enough. But if you want, you're welcome."

"Thanks."

Jim slows as they come to a six-car pile-up. Black crows flap up from the coloured wreckage on their approach. In the centre of the wreck a bloodied body lies half out a shattered windscreen.

"Carrion," Jim says, drives slowly by on the hard shoulder.

"Who'd have thought a week ago," Herbie says, "we'd all end up like this?"

"All this morning," Jim works up through the gears, "all bloody day yesterday, I kept looking around me and thinking, Is it now? While she was talking to me about the farmers and the milk, I looked at the jamjars in her hand and I thought, Is it now? I looked at the kitchen clock, Is it now? Even last night, when I had those three jacks, pissed as I was, there I was hoping it wouldn't come before I laid 'em. That wreck back there too."

"Know what you mean. Maybe that's why I'm down. I had to have him before it came. Now I've got him ... Let it come."

They drive in silence.

Both look over to the lorry that has been abandoned in the other carriageway. Run out of diesel, they decided when they passed it on their way down to Southampton.

"Think the lead up to a nuclear war would've been like this?" Jim says.

"No." Herbie thinks. "No. Nowhere near as bad. You'd have got some, like now, who'd have gone potty. But they'd have been a minority. And we'd have been going to war. We'd have had a war mentality. Disloyalty, duty and all that. And you'd have had plenty who'd be thinking they'd call it off at the last minute. Then you'd get others thinking they'd be the ones who'd survive. And the police and the ambulance and the hospitals, they'd all have definite jobs to do. And the feeling that it may not happen. But this … This is … implacable."

Jim decelerates as they come in sight of a single wreck tangled in the central barrier.

"Step on it. Eh, Jim."

Saturday: 17:18

Sal meets him in the hall, "Can't come in the kitchen."

Herbie turns towards the living room. Sal quickly bars that door. "Not in there either."

"Where," Herbie grins down on her, "am I supposed to go then? Back outside?"

"Upstairs." Sal pushes him towards the stairs. "You finished the job?"

"Filed my report. In triplicate. Kept the car, though."

"You're on holiday now, then. So you can go up and have a shower, change your clothes."

"You're the boss."

Loosening his tie Herbie starts mock obediently up the stairs. "How's your Mum?"

"Oh … In a bad way."

"Yeah?" Herbie stops.

"No. Not Mum." Sal says. "You know Mum. It's this girl next door."

"What girl next door?"

"They haven't been there that long. But, poor cow, she's seven months pregnant. I can see why Mum feels so sorry for her."

"Taken her under her wing?"

"Not exactly. No, she's more like, well, obsessed by her. I must admit it's a bit eerie."

"How d'you mean?"

"She's gone into a sort of trance. Girl next door, that is. Just sits there. Doesn't say a thing. Her husband, nobody, can get a single word out of her. She's not eating. Just sits there, hands on her stomach. It's very weird."

"All day?"

"Last couple of days. She got up to go to the toilet once while I was there. Everybody's watching her. Her husband's taken the lock off the bathroom door. Locked herself in yesterday. For two hours, Mum said. He had to get a ladder, break the window. And they got two other children. They were crying. They're in Mum's most of the time now. Nice little boy. Bit frightened of their mother, though. And the stink's terrible over there. Rubbish all over the forecourt."

The cooker buzzer sounds in the kitchen. Sal starts down the hall. "Anyway, he's taken the lock off the bathroom door. Mum sends her love. Don't you come down now," Sal raises her voice, "until I call you. Promise?"

"Promise."

'The trouble with Time Travel is that you inevitably end up in a Time Loop – from every future going back to ensure your own existence.'

Barry Popieluszko. Happy Robot Goes Cosmic: Fire Dragon.

'All life is selfish in its desire to survive.'

Barry Popieluszko. Psychotic Android Eats: Fire Dragon.

Saturday: 22:13

Sal reaches the phone first. "Julie? … Yes. Hello darling … Oh, well done! Worth the trip? … Oh well, it's the journey that matters, they say … Did you? … I've been cooking practically all day … No, I enjoyed it. I went round your Gran's this morning. She sends her love … Doesn't seem to bother her in the least … Maybe it won't … Yes … I love you too, darling … I've been so proud of you … Yes … Maybe it won't … I've loved you so much … Sorry."

Weeping, she thrusts the phone at Herbie.

"Julie?"

Tears are being suppressed. "Dad?"

"Your Mum beat me to it tonight. She cooked us a cordon bleu. Candles, the lot. I reckon it was a deliberate ploy on her part. So she'd get to the phone first. I'm so full I can hardly breathe. You've made it, then?"

"We're in Naples now."

"Good girl. Seems like we Watkins always achieve our objectives. The international sleuth Herbie Watkins today successfully solved his last case."

"I could've done with some of Mum's cooking." The tears are under control now. "We've been living on pizzas and pastas. Pizzas are as thick as cakes here."

"No trouble getting food, then?"

"Quite a few places have reopened. Seems like everyone's had their fling, wants to get back to normal now."

"We're all still here."

"True. Dad?"

"Yeah?"

"Dad, I love you. Thanks for everything."

"I should be thanking you. For what you've given us."

In Naples there are tears again.

"Don't cry, love. May never happen."

"Oh Dad." Laughter bubbles down the line.

"We've been looking through all the old photos," Herbie says. "Had some laughs."

"Least I won't be embarrassed by them anymore."

"What you got planned for tomorrow?"

"Thought we'd go to Pompeii." A sniff. "Seems appropriate. Get into the spirit of the thing. We've got some wine, a couple of glasses. And some very ripe camembert. Thought we'd have a picnic up there."

"Sounds like a good idea. Can I speak to Peter?"

"OK."

Herbie hears indistinct words, the telephone being passed over.

"Hello?"

"Peter?"

"Yes?"

"Well done. You made it."

"Yes."

"Got enough money to get back if it doesn't happen?"

"I think so."

"If you haven't, go to the local consul, get them to ring me."

"OK."

"Where you staying tonight? Got a hotel?"

"We're camping out. Sitting on the rim of Vesuvius."

"Ain't we all."

"Julie's all right, Mr Watkins. A bit upset, that's all."

"I know, Peter. Thanks."

Sal taps Herbie's arm for the phone.

"Hold on," Herbie says, gives the phone to Sal.

"Peter? … I want to thank you for taking care of Julie … I was a bit put out when you came here. Took me by surprise … Thank you … Bless you, boy …"

The phone is pushed back at Herbie.

"Hello?"

"Dad?"

"You all right now?"

"Tell Mum not to worry, Dad."

"I will. For all the good it'll do."

"We're almost out of change now. It's a money gobbler this thing. Poor old Peter's got a sore thumb pushing it in. We thought we had masses too. Sorry, Dad."

"You need never apologise to me."

The line goes dead. Herbie weeps.

'God was the elastic in my underpants. He let me down.'
                              Graffiti. Princess Street, Newcastle upon Tyne.

'Time's going back to all zeros.'
                              Barry Popieluszko. Raw As Birth: White Swan.

Sunday: 10:10

Facing the bathroom mirror Herbie pats on aftershave, pauses to once more press down a tuft of sleep-twisted hair. He listens.

The church bells have stopped.

"Breakfast's ready," Sal calls up the stairs.

Herbie leaves the bathroom, slops down the stairs in his slippers. He has on an open-necked check shirt, brown cardigan, old grey slacks.

The kitchen is empty.

"Out here." Sal waves to him from the garden.

The strip of garden ends in a wooden slat fence. A washing line loops along above the straight concrete path. On either side of the concrete path is cropped lawn. Along the dark brown fences Sal's flowerbeds bloom red and white.

Sal has brought out one of the small living room tables, has covered it with a white tablecloth. Silver teapot, white cups, saucers, jug of milk, sugar bowl, plates, toast rack, pots of jam and marmalade – all sparkle in the bright morning sun.

"Slowcoach," Sal says, pours the tea gleaming brown like varnish out of the silver spout. Herbie stoops to place a kiss against Sal's lifted cheek, sits opposite her. The chair wobbles.

Once settled he rasps butter thickly over a triangle of toast, spreads orange-glinting marmalade upon it, takes a bite.

No traffic, no jets, no voices, no radio, no birdsong, no buzz of insects. He looks to Sal. She is looking quizzically to him.

So does this universe end – not with a bang, nor with a whimper, but in expectant silence.

Also Available from BeWrite Books

www.bewrite.net

Marks
by Sam Smith

Life for country detective George Hawkins is a daily, clockwork routine of petty reports, small-time embezzlement and sleazy divorce.

To save overnight stake-outs, shivering in his car, he chalks a line on a car tyre and roadway. The following morning, if the marks still match up, it's proof enough that a car has not been moved, and someone has been playing away from home.

But then – in the space of a few short hours – he must turn a blind eye to a callous hit-and-run, his home is targeted by a burglar with more on his mind than robbing a few knick-knacks, and his girlfriend mysteriously disappears without a trace.

While zealous local police – obsessed with proving his guilt as a murderer – investigate him, George is forced into two investigations of his own that will change his life forever … one into a network of ruthless, high-tech industrial spies and another into his own heart and mind.

As the plot twists and turns, new questions are posed by every answer, and the pre-conceived ideas and prejudices planted by his father – a former Japanese prisoner of war on the killer Burma railroad – are turned on their head.

In this baffling, psychological tangle, George no longer knows who is friend and who is foe.

And the chalk marks he used to make to prove the guilt of overnight adulterers, no longer match up in his own life.

Print ISBN 1-904224-09-1
eBook ISBN 1-904224-02-4

Porlock Counterpoint
by Sam Smith

There are criminals … and there are **criminals!**

Where sit the guilty? Around your dinner table? Grubbing for pennies on a street corner? Where does poor innocence cross the line? When does 'middle-class' become sordid?

In this sprint-paced, intriguing book of words, Sam Smith poses these questions.

He suggests there is a difference between good and bad … depending only from which standpoint you examine the scene of the crime.

Like a master crossword-puzzle compiler … he lays a trail of clues to your own private stance and leaves you to find the only fitting answer for yourself.

A luckless young couple with a baby on the way stumble onto a treasure-trove drug dump when they joy-ride an expensive car to the maternity hospital … in desperation.

A rich, middle-aged yuppie couple with a private yacht, a home in the country and their very own drugs ring count their money … in their own kind of innocence.

Porlock Counterpoint explores the descant between the two couples and explodes the myth of attraction of opposites. Each couple detests the morals and social status of the other.

The earthy detectives on their trail despise them both … they even despise each other!

They all play in counterpoint.

Sam Smith is the skilled questionmaster. The reader decides who's on the side of the angels.

Print ISBN 1-904224-15-6
eBook ISBN 1-904224-14-8

The Care Vortex
by Sam Smith

A group of teenaged girls in a penny-pinching privately owned care institution struggle to come to terms with their pasts – and their futures.

Meanwhile, care workers at Bridge House struggle to come to terms with the girls themselves and the horrors of their earlier lives.

In the face of ineptitude, indifference and greed, dedicated – but weary – care worker, Barry Gresham, faces the effects of child prostitution, drug addiction, self-mutilation, domestic incest, violence, and crime against heavy establishment odds … and also against the cynical opposition of his life-hardened young charges.

Sam Smith's gripping and disturbingly real novel explodes comfortable myths and exposes a care vortex into which youngsters often vanish without trace.

Drawing on several years of observation and research, Smith writes with undeniable authority. His characters become starkly real as he works through their coldly official case histories and follows the girls and Barry through the volatile days and nights of a single working shift.

The Care Vortex is an irresistible, no-holds-barred, page-turner of a novel in its own right. But it is also a vital reality check – a wake-up call that will rouse every reader.

(All Smith's royalties from the sale of this book are to be donated to the charity, Child Aid Direct)

Print ISBN 1-904224-44-4
eBook ISBN 1-904224-98-9

Vera & Eddy's War
by Sam Smith

Vera and Eddy were just one working-class couple among millions caught up in the fury of the Second World War.

Later, they used to talk and talk of their experiences. One day author Sam Smith decided to listen.

This remarkable book is the result of countless recorded interviews with Vera and Eddy, his in-laws, and paints an unforgettably human and strikingly real picture of how two small people emerged, scorched but complete, from the flames of the bloodiest conflict in the history of mankind.

Vera and Eddy lead us through the pain and the outlandish, sometimes ghoulish humour, the desperate hopes and stark terrors of times when doorsteps and cinemas, invasion beaches and battlefields were all equally in the front line.

Days when uncertainty was a constant companion and mutilation and death were never more than a moment away.

So expertly does Smith apply his no-frills narrative style, that the reader can *hear* the shattering explosions as pregnant Vera dodges the bombs blitzing her streets, and *feel* the hot breath of shrapnel whipping past Eddy's ears in the killing zones of Normandy and Holland.

Smith's book reads as one of the most gripping, frantically paced war novels ever written.

What elevates it from the merely great to the truly magnificent is that every single word is true.

Print ISBN 1-904224-97-0

Sick Ape
by Sam Smith

The Sick Ape of the title dwells in the mind. Although that's not the first consideration of this tale.

First there's the accident of meeting of two divorced and embittered fathers, then comes a cooking and eating of meals, followed by a marriage of disgruntled minds.

The consequence of which leads to the pair of them getting labelled terrorists – all within a book dedicated to non-terrorists – with them finally, and during, seeking to resolve their campaign in different ways. One being death. One being this book.

Print ISBN 1-904492-17-7
eBook ISBN 1-904492-15-0

Also Available from BeWrite Books

Crime
The Knotted Cord — Alistair Kinnon
The Tangled Skein — Alistair Kinnon
Scent of Crime — Linda Stone

Crime/Humour
Sweet Molly Maguire — Terry Houston

Horror
Chill — Terri Pine, Peter Lee, Andrew Müller

Fantasy/Humour
Zolin A Rockin' Good Wizard — Barry Ireland
The Hundredfold Problem — John Grant
Earthdoom! — David Langford & John Grant

Fantasy
The Far-Enough Window — John Grant
A Season of Strange Dreams — C. S. Thompson
And Then the Night — C. S. Thompson

Collections/ Short Stories
As the Crow Flies — Dave Hutchinson
The Loss of Innocence — Jay Mandal
Kaleidoscope — Various
Odie Dodie — Lad Moore
Tailwind — Lad Moore
The Miller Moth — Mike Broemmel
The Shadow Cast — Mike Broemmel
As the Crow Flies — Dave Hutchinson
The Creature in the Rose — Various

Thriller
Deep Ice — Karl Kofoed
Blood Money — Azam Gill
Evil Angel — RD Larson
Disremembering Eddie — Anne Morgellyn
Flight to Pakistan — Azam Gill
Removing Edith Mary — Anne Morgellyn

Historical Fiction
Ring of Stone — Hugh McCracken
Jahred and The Magi — Wilma Clark
The Kinnons of Candleriggs — Jenny Telfer Chaplin
Treason — Meredith Whitford

Contemporary
Someplace Like Home — Terrence Moore
A Tangle of Roots — David Hough

Whispers of Ghosts   Ron McLachlan

Young Adult
Rules of the Hunt   Hugh McCracken
The Time Drum   Hugh McCracken
Kitchen Sink Concert   Ishbel Moore
The Fat Moon Dance   Elizabeth Taylor
Grandfather and The Ghost   Hugh McCracken
Return from the Hunt   Hugh McCracken

Children's
The Secret Portal   Reno Charlton
The Vampire Returns   Reno Charlton

Autobiography/Biography
A Stranger and Afraid   Arthur Allwright

Poetry
A Moment for Me   Heather Grace
Shaken & Stirred   Various
Letters from Portugal   Jan Oskar Hansen
Routes   Twelve poets. A road less traveled.
Vinegar Moon   Donna Biffar
The Drowning Fish   John G Hall
listen to the geckos...   tolulope ogunlesi

General
The Wounded Stone   Terry Houston
Magpies and Sunsets   Neil Alexander Marr
Redemption of Quapaw Mountain Bertha Sutliff

Romance
A Different Kind of Love   Jay Mandal
The Dandelion Clock   Jay Mandal

Humour
The Cuckoos of Batch Magna   Peter Maughan

Science Fiction
Gemini Turns   Anne Marie Duquette

Adventure
Matabele Gold   Michael J Hunt
The African Journals of
Petros Amm   Michael J Hunt
The Stones of Petronicus   Peter Tomlinson

Printed in the United Kingdom
by Lightning Source UK Ltd.
114070UKS00001B/4-12